HOLLY BERRIES AND HOCKEY PUCKS

A DICKENS HOLIDAY ROMANCE

LUCINDA RACE

Happy Holidays
xo
Lucinda

MC TWO PRESS

INSPIRATION

May your home be filled with happiness and love today and always

CHAPTER 1

$\mathcal{T}$he door to Jillian Morgan's shop slammed open with a blast of cold October wind. The large white bucket of flowers, which only moments before had been held in her hands, hit the floor. To make matters worse, water sloshed across the floor and soaked her tennis shoes. It wasn't even eight, and this was not the way to start a day. She brushed a wayward curl out of her eyes, and even though she wasn't open yet, she smiled at the potential customer standing in front of her. The only saving grace was that he had remained dry.

"Good morning. How can I help you?"

He pointed to the door over his shoulder. "I just saw your closed sign." The man was close to six feet tall and slender, with short dirty-blond hair and hazel eyes. He gave her a sheepish smile. "I can come back."

"No, it's fine." She didn't remember seeing him in her shop before and wondered if he was just passing through town.

He bent over and retrieved the bucket. "Looks like your day isn't off to a great start." His smile was bright and

1

friendly. "If you get a mop, I'll clean up the water and you can save the flowers."

"No, that's alright, but thank you." She stepped over the puddle to stand behind the counter and brushed back another stray curl. "How can I help you today?"

He looked at the flowers still on the floor and flashed her a grin. "Tell you what. Let me help you clean this up, really, and I'll give you my flower order." He tipped his head to the side. "And for my trouble, you can give me ten percent off."

Since he insisted on being a nice guy, she relented. "I'm Jillian, owner of this shop." She wasn't used to someone offering extraneous help with much of anything, and that included raising her daughter, Melanie. After a moment of hesitation, she said, "Thank you."

He stuck out his hand. "I'm Brett and I've only lived in town for a couple of months."

That kind of explained why she hadn't seen him before. Besides, between running the shop and spending as much time as she could with Melanie, she didn't socialize much. There just weren't enough hours in the day. "Welcome to Dickens. And you're just in time for the holiday season. From Labor Day until the New Year, we're always up to something around here, but mostly it's all about Christmas, considering the name of our little town."

"It's charming. Even though I grew up near Boston, my parents used to bring me to the tree lighting ceremony here every year."

She leaned against the counter. "I think that's one of my favorite nights during the holiday season. It's magical." She could hear the wistful tone in her voice and snapped back to florist mode. "Do you have any idea what you'd like today for an arrangement?"

Brett began to pick up flowers and set them in the now upright five-gallon bucket. "I'm not sure. Something bright and cheery, maybe with some daisies." He held up a lily. "And whatever this is?"

She suppressed a grin. He looked cute with his hands full of flowers dripping water. "I can include some daisies *and* lilies in the arrangement. Are there any other flowers you'd like?" He continued to fill the bucket with flowers from the floor until the last ones had been scooped up. "Why don't you look around and see if any of the arrangements in the cooler strike you, or I'm happy to put together something new."

She hurried through the archway into the back room, where she grabbed the mop and floor bucket. When she came back into the main shop area, Brett was studying each prearranged bouquet with great interest.

"Did you make all of these morning?"

She dropped the wet mop into the squeeze part and wrung it out and proceeded to wipe up the last of the puddle. "Actually, last night." She pushed the mop and bucket back into the storage room and when she returned, she asked, "Did you find something?"

He gestured to an arrangement that had white roses, lilies, and colorful Gerber daisies. "I like this one. These are much prettier than the supermarket flowers I've been buying." He winced. "Sorry. I've been meaning to come in sooner."

"I'm glad you're here now." She pulled it from the case and pointed to the cards on the counter. "I can have it delivered by lunchtime. If you want to add a card, help yourself."

"Can I take it with me? I'd like to personally deliver it."

She gave him a smile. "The personal touch is always appreciated." She slipped the vase into a protective wrapper and stapled the top. "Is there anything else I can get you?"

"Would it be possible to have an arrangement made up for me each week for the rest of the year? Similar size, but make them with different color schemes each week, and for the holidays, can you create themed arrangements in seasonal colors? Oh, and do you know where I can get a few wreaths?"

3

"Sure, I can do all of that. Same day and time each week?"

"Yes, please."

She pulled out her order pad and made notes about the upcoming orders. She was pleased to have the job. "Right before Thanksgiving, I'll have wreaths for sale and if you'd like, I am accepting preorders now."

He pulled out his wallet to pay for the flowers. "Put me down for two large wreaths and if I could pick up the arrangements every Wednesday around four thirty, that would be good."

How sweet. He must have a weekly dinner with his girlfriend. She wondered if Heather, her best friend and owner of the Library Cat Bookstore, might have some idea about this new hunk in town and who he might be dating. "I can definitely do that." She handed him a business card. "I close at five but if there is any time when you're running late, just give me a call and we can figure something out so you'll still be able to pick them up."

"Thanks. That's really nice of you."

She ran his credit card and handed him the electronic pad to sign. "Thank you for your business." She cringed at how perky her voice was, but a steady customer, not just for the bouquets but wreaths too, was a nice boost for the rest of the year. "One last question. Will you want the flowers in vases each week or will you want to reuse the one you have with today's arrangement?"

He picked up the flowers and glanced at the clear cut glass vase. "This is pretty and multipurpose but for next week, let's have another vase. That way they can be washed in between."

"Perfect."

He gave her a warm smile that made the gold in his eyes sparkle. "Jillian, I'll see you next Wednesday."

With that, he was gone. She leaned against the counter and watched as he disappeared down the street. He was handsome. Not that she needed a complication of the male variety.

Her cell pinged. It was her mom. Her daughter was asking if they were still going to the skating rink tonight. There were signups for hockey and she was determined to make the team.

Without hesitation, she answered, *Yes*. She wanted her daughter to gain the same sense of confidence on the ice she'd had as a kid. Hockey had given her more than just confidence; it had helped pay her way through college, and that's where she had met Melanie's father, even if he had turned out to be an absentee dad. He was chasing the dream of becoming financially successful and maybe someday he'd figure out she was worth more than a monthly check, fancy gifts for special occasions, and an occasional phone call and an even rarer visit. The last time he had seen her was almost four years ago.

*B*rett carried the vase of flowers to his car. A smile played over his face. Jillian was a surprise; he hadn't expected the owner of Petals to be a pretty young woman who jolted his heart into action. It had been a while since Racine had broken off their engagement and he had no interest in getting involved with anyone new, but it felt good to appreciate the pretty woman with cornflower-blue eyes and blond curls. She was the picture of the girl next door and he was already looking forward to next Wednesday. But first a quick stop at his mom's work, and then he had signed up to start coaching the local youth hockey team and tonight was the first practice.

"Mom, where are you?" He walked through the empty kitchen and carried the vase into the living room, where his mom was sitting in his father's recliner, a box of tissues on her lap and discarded ones littering the floor.

5

Setting the vase of flowers on the coffee table, he said, "Hey, Mom." His voice was gentle as he dropped to one knee and touched her hand. "What's going on?" His heart was cement in his chest.

Her hazel eyes were rimmed red and bloodshot. "Brett, when did you get here? I must have lost track of time."

"Just now." He pointed to the table. "Surprise."

She patted a hand over her chic-styled silvery-blond hair and placed a freckled hand against his cheek. "Are those for me?"

"They are. I finally made time to investigate the flower shop and I just had to pick some up. Dad always bought you flowers." A fresh wave a grief washed over him as he remembered all the Wednesdays his dad had come home carrying a bright bouquet for her.

"Your father brought me a bouquet every week all the years we were married."

"I remember sometimes he picked wildflowers. I think those were some of your favorites."

Her eyes got a faraway look. "Before we moved to Dickens, we had that huge flower garden where I could cut them every day. Every table in our home had vases of colorful blooms during the summer."

"And Dad bought different flowers every week." He handed her a tissue.

She dried her cheeks. "I'm glad you came over today, and thank you for the flowers. They're lovely, but you should find a special girl you can buy flowers for every week, and not your mother." A sad smile graced her mouth.

"Mom, I don't have time to date. I'm still unpacking my apartment and getting used to my new job." He eased back on the sofa. "But I did make a call to the youth hockey club. At work, someone mentioned they were looking for an assistant coach." He gave a one-shouldered shrug. "I thought it'd be good to get back on the ice."

"Is this a pre-Christmas miracle?" Mom flashed him a genuinely pleased smile. "You haven't held a hockey stick in over ten years."

"I don't want to rehash the past, Mom, but I can still skate, and who knows? Maybe there's a kid that would be interested in learning from me." He got up and grabbed a small trash can. "I'll clean this up, but I do need to get to work. Any chance you'd want to make meatloaf tomorrow night for dinner, with baby carrots and all the good stuff?"

She shook a finger at him. "I know you have an ulterior motive to get me off the chair, but how can I say no to my favorite son asking for his favorite meal, and in the middle of the week?"

"I'm your only kid, so I'd better be your favorite." He dropped a kiss on her cheek. "If you need anything before tomorrow, give me a call."

She stood up and gave him a hard hug. "Be patient with me."

He could hear the catch in her voice. "I will. Everyone says the first year is the hardest. But you've got me and we'll get through all the firsts together." He held her tight, his chin resting on top of her head. "I think we should go out for Thanksgiving dinner. There's plenty of time to make a reservation." He didn't want to tell her he already had. "We'll talk about it tomorrow night."

"I'm not sure, but I'll think about it." She released him with a final squeeze. "Thanks for stopping. I woke up feeling blue and you added a sparkle to my day."

"Why don't you go to the library today, and tomorrow the market? Or better yet, you could stop at that little bookstore in town. You might meet some people."

"Brett, you're pushing me again." She gave him a small poke "You need to get to work and I have a shopping list to make."

"I'll call you later."

"You'll do no such thing; you don't need to hover. Besides, you have hockey practice tonight."

This time, the smile reached her eyes and his internal knot relaxed.

"That's something I haven't said in a long time. Have fun." She opened the kitchen door and ushered him out. "See you at six tomorrow." She closed the door behind him, effectively pushing him along.

His parents had moved to Dickens in January, and his dad had been diagnosed with cancer in March. He'd been with his father in the final weeks of his life and had helped take care of him. It was only after his dad passed that he had found a job and officially moved to Dickens. And now, it had been four months and he was learning to live without his rock. Sadly, there hadn't been time for his mom to make new friends or find a support network before Dad had gotten so sick. Hopefully today would be the first step if she'd go the bookstore or library; one thing she had always loved was to read.

He looked back at the one-story house where his parents had planned to spend their retirement years and his heart ached for what would never be. Life rarely turned out as you planned and Brett knew that firsthand. His dream career and his engagement were both like wisps of smoke, gone with the wind.

CHAPTER 2

"I can't wait to go to hockey." Melanie flopped on the floor. "Will all this stuff fit in my bag?"

Jillian sat cross-legged on the floor next to the open gear bag, tired from a busy day in the shop. She had never really gotten into a good groove after dumping the bucket of flowers in front of her new customer, Brett.

So far, Melanie's skates were inside along with her helmet, pads, face mask, socks, pants, and gloves. She searched the two inside pockets. She found Mel's pelvic protector. "Kiddo, where's your mouthpiece container?"

Melanie shrugged. "I dunno." She looked around and hopped up from the floor. "I see it." She grabbed it off the bed and giggled as she made a wild toss to Jillian, who caught it by stretching to the right.

Jillian decided not to admonish her about throwing things in the house tonight.

Melanie clapped her hands. "You caught it!" Her laugh filled the room. "Gram says I'm gonna be a Mite. She says you were a Mite too."

"I was. All kids who are under eight are considered Mites and in a couple of years, you'll move up to Squirt."

She scrunched up her nose. "Those are funny names."

"They are, but when you grow up and become a famous hockey player…"

"Like you were, Momma?" Her head tilted to one side and it was easy to see the excitement in her eyes. "Gram tells me stories about each trophy she has in your old room. She says you were a big deal."

"I wasn't famous, honey. My college team won a championship and we all worked hard to make it happen."

"But Gram says you were the captain and everyone liked you."

"That was a long time ago. Now it's your turn to learn the basics and become a good team player. That's critical for the success of any team."

Melanie crossed her arms over her chest and dropped her chin. "What if the boys don't want to let me play? Some of the kids at school said only boys are on the team and I'll be the only girl."

Jillian's heart twinged. "I don't think you'll be the only girl; that's just kids talking." She remembered that very same fear. She scooted across the floor and folded her arms around her mini-me, from the blond curls and blue of her eyes to the small dimple in her cheek. There was nothing of her tall, dark, and very handsome father in this little girl, and that was a good thing. The last thing she wanted was another reminder of the man who up and left his daughter without so much as a second thought.

"I'm going to tell you the same thing Gram told me every time I began to work with a new team," she said. "Work hard, play hard, but most of all, have fun. That's what playing a sport is all about. If you're not having fun, it's not worth it."

Melanie looked at Jillian, her eyes wide. "Does that mean I don't have to keep playing if I don't like it?"

Jillian shook her head. "Bug, you know our house rule. If you make a commitment, you have to honor it, and you're agreeing to be on the Dickens Drummers team, so you'll last the entire season. If you decide you don't want to play next year, you don't have to. Deal?"

Melanie gave her mom's hand one shake. "Deal."

"Finish getting ready and I'll meet you in the living room, and don't forget to use the bathroom."

The little girl scrambled up from the bedroom floor and raced down the hall. The bathroom door banged shut. Jillian zipped up the gear bag. She could picture Melanie cruising around the ice. At least she didn't need to learn how to skate or the proper way to hold the stick. Jillian hadn't wanted to push her to play, but she had gotten excited when Melanie told her about the sign in the town square she had seen when Gram picked her up from school. She loved to be on the ice just as much as Jillian did, and they skated every chance they got on Grosvenors Pond each winter. This would be the first time Jillian had stepped foot in a rink since she had walked away from an opportunity to play on the Olympic team. At one time she had thought she'd be a college coach or even work with men's hockey. The day she took the test and saw the pink plus sign, her life had changed and there was no looking back.

She heard the water running in the sink and slung the gear bag over her shoulder. From experience, she knew she needed another layer of clothes. Ice rinks were freaking cold, especially when you weren't skating.

*C*ars filled the parking lot and Jillian eased her Outback into what looked to be the last free space near the road. There had to be kids from neighboring towns who had also come to sign up. At least this wasn't a tryout; with this group, every kid was included. There was a natural cutting process. Once parents understood the time commitment—practice twice a week and one game on the weekend

—kids would melt away. After that, the next group of kids who'd rather be in front of a screen and didn't want to be in the rink would evaporate. That would leave the coaches with the best group.

"Momma, come on. We gotta get inside. Look at how many people came." Melanie's seat belt was off and her car door was open.

"I'll get your bag and stick."

"I'll carry it; it's got all my stuff." Melanie dragged the bag across the back seat. It landed on the hard ground with a thud. "Got it." She slammed the car door and struggled to get the strap across her body and heave it off the ground.

Jillian suppressed a grin as she watched Melanie stagger. She was one determined little girl. Jillian held up the bag to help her and took the stick too. Locking the car, they crossed the parking lot. Once the leaves were off the trees, the ground would soon be coated with snow—if the weather forecast was correct. Thanksgiving was just four weeks away, and then Christmas. Jillian was trying to get tickets for a professional hockey game as a gift for her and Melanie but so far, the ticket prices were just too high. She might take her to a college game instead.

Melanie adjusted the strap on her shoulder.

"Sure you don't want me to carry that for you?" Jillian opened the heavy steel door to the rink.

"Nope. I got it."

In the small vestibule, signs indicated which age group should go where. The sign for Mites pointed to the left. They entered a large lobby with parents and kids alike all talking and milling around. Doors led to the stands, with one door leading directly onto the ice. She looked to the left and saw the sign for the locker rooms. A few kids were chasing each other around the room, and she was relieved to see some girls as well as boys. She nudged Melanie's shoulder and gestured to a little girl with long braids.

"Isn't that Suzi from your class?"

Melanie nodded but didn't say anything. Instead, she stood quietly, taking it all in. "Do you think they all want to be a Mite?"

A hint of doubt had crept into her voice. Her hand slipped into Jillian's and held on tight. She gave it an encouraging squeeze.

"You skate like the wind and you have some basics down pat."

She saw a spot on the far side of the room where they could wait and steered Melanie in that direction. They threaded their way through the groups of families, both large and small. She carried the bag and stick so Melanie wouldn't knock into anyone.

An older man walked into the room wearing a dark-blue knit cap and a fleece with the Dickens Drummers logo. Jillian recognized Coach Richards; he had been her coach when she was young. Another man, close to six feet tall and lanky, walked in behind him. He looked familiar and when his eyes locked with hers, they widened in mild surprise. It was her customer from the shop today. Brett.

🏒

*T*he minute Brett scanned the room, his eyes found the beautiful florist. Standing next to her was a cute curly-headed girl. He wouldn't have guessed he would have found her in a hockey rink. Maybe there wasn't much else to do for the winter months, or maybe the little girl's mom was a hockey fan. He gave her a smile, which she returned.

Coach Richards gave a welcoming speech and with a chuckle, said, "If anyone is looking for the basketball courts, they're on the opposite side of the parking lot."

A ripple of laughter slid from one side of the room to the other.

"We're going to divide into several groups by age. Seven- and eight-year-olds, line up under the purple banner. Next group, ages nine through twelve, under the red banner, and anyone who is six and under, gather near the blue Mites banner. Coach Parsons will meet you there."

Brett walked over to Jillian and the little girl.

"Hello. It's nice to see you again."

She placed her hands on her daughter's shoulders. "This is my daughter, Melanie."

He knelt down to look her in the eyes. "Nice to meet you. I'm Coach Parsons. Are you signing up to play?"

"Uh-huh. I got all my gear too." She tipped her head. "Can girls play on your team?"

"Sure can." He looked at Jillian, who smiled at him, and then back at Melanie. "Can you skate?"

"Yup. Momma says I'm like the wind."

"That will help on the ice." He had to chuckle to himself. Jillian was already looking to be a good hockey mom. She was prepared and warmly dressed for sitting on the sidelines.

Coach Richards stood in front of the group. "Hello, parents and players. I'd like to introduce Coach Parsons. He's new in town, so be nice to him. I'm asking him to kick things off for us today."

Brett addressed the group. "Hello, everyone. For those of you who've not been here before, always check the board when you come in to see which locker room you're assigned to. Everyone needs to be in full gear, including mouth and neck guards, or I can't let you on the ice. Today we'll see how everyone skates, but we won't be using our sticks. So get your gear on and I'll see you on the ice."

Out of the corner of his eye, he saw Melanie grab her bag strap and grin at her mom. He already was impressed with the girl; she was independent, but would that translate to a good team player long term? With a shriek of his whistle, the group moved to the door. Jillian held Melanie back to let some kids go ahead of her. Was she nervous to have her daughter on the ice?

They stopped near him and Brett said, "Are you ready to have some fun?"

She flashed him a grateful smile and tipped her head toward Melanie. "Someone's a little nervous."

"Understandable. I'm guessing this is your first year."

Melanie shook her head. "No, I play with Momma at the pond."

"Well, hopefully I can teach you something too." He directed them to the far side of the locker room, where he helped Melanie set her bag on the bench. He couldn't help but notice Jillian glance at the ice as they walked to the locker room. Her face almost looked wistful. He took a quick look around and wondered where this bright-eyed little girl's dad was sitting.

He noticed Melanie's gear bag. It looked brand new, which Brett knew was an expensive outlay. If the rest of her equipment was new, he'd have to suggest to Jillian to network with other parents for used equipment. Kids grew so fast that it made sense to pass things along to the up-and-comers and next time, she wouldn't have such a huge cash outlay.

A while later, he was surprised to see Melanie easily gliding over the ice and Jillian clapping her hands, encouraging her to turn and pick up speed. There was more to this hockey mom than he knew and he was going to enjoy discovering her secrets.

CHAPTER 3

*A*fter Melanie got into her gear, she hit the ice. Some kids were free skating before practice; others were warming the bench. Jillian watched as Melanie made the turn at the end of the rink and skated toward her at full speed. She stopped with a swivel of her body so her skates could bite into the ice, sending a small spray in Jillian's direction.

She called out, "That looked good. How did it feel, Melanie?"

"It was fun." Melanie looked around at some of the other kids who were struggling to stay upright. But she never gloated. In fact, when Suzi's legs went out from under her and she landed hard on the ice, Melanie said, "I'm going to go help Suzi." Then she took off.

Jillian stuck her hands in her coat pockets and discovered she forgot to put the pocket warmers in. When she looked up, she noticed Brett was watching her before his eyes followed Melanie across the ice. She took a modicum of satisfaction at the look of surprise on his face at her daughter's ability. She was a natural and came by it honestly. Brett gave her a half nod with a smile.

Coach Richards blew his whistle and motioned for the kids to circle around. Parents began to move into the stands, but Jillian leaned against the rink wall and watched Brett. Did this guy have a clue about coaching? That was the mystery. She ran her gaze over him, noting his zip-front jacket and black pants. From head to toe, he had the look of a coach. He was in great shape, which she had noticed before, but on the ice, he had a swagger about him. He was comfortable on skates, like they were a part of him. Within a few minutes, he had the kids separated in what she thought was a haphazard grouping and asked them to skate the width of the rink and back.

Jillian caught his eye as he glanced at the stands and back at her. She longed to feel her blades bite into the ice as she drove the puck to the net. It was as if she could hear the hollow thud of sticks banging on the boards as the team celebrated a goal. But this wasn't about her. This was Melanie's time to shine.

*B*rett watched as Jillian settled into the stands, but her eyes never left the ice. The look on her face was almost wistful. It was as if she belonged there. Maybe she had been a figure skater. He had been in hockey skates since he was four and he knew what it was like to relish the crunch of skates on the frozen surface.

He noticed Melanie was comfortable on the ice, but could she handle a puck and would she be afraid of a pack of kids all chasing her if she was the one driving it? He had to be careful; he was already looking out for a single player. He took one last glance at Jillian and gave her an awkward glove-covered thumbs-up, trying to convey it was going well.

The hour was up and their time on the ice was over for

tonight. He pulled the kids together for the head coach's rousing pep talk at the end of practice. When Coach Richards was finished, Brett said, "I hope to see you all here next week when we start our regular practice on Monday." He was going to pass out the schedules, but some kids were barely staying on their feet. "I'll give your parents our schedule."

Melanie tentatively raised her hand.

"Yes, Melanie?"

Her voice was soft. "Coach, will we get to use our sticks with the puck next time?"

Halfway through her mumbled question, she took her mouth guard out so he understood the last part.

Brett contained his grin.

Coach Richards said, "Probably not. We'll have to see how things are going."

Her shoulders slumped. He hated to see any kid disappointed, but for some reason, he wanted to buoy up her spirits.

He skated over to her. "Melanie, have you played much hockey?"

Her angelic face was covered with the face cage. "Momma and I played on the pond last winter. I can't wait to play in here." Her face lit up as her gaze roamed the rink. "This is so much bigger."

With a chuckle, he said, "It is, but we'll be using half the ice for practice and another team will be on the other side."

There was nothing worse than having kids sitting on the bench, waiting for ice time. Boredom always spelled trouble. Kids horsing around and with sharp skates on their feet and weapons in their hands in the form of hockey sticks meant it was easy for them to hurt each other.

"I can't wait for our next practice." She grinned and nodded. "Can I go tell my mom now?"

He nodded. "That's it for today, kids. See you all next

week and great job today!" He high-fived each kid as they filed past him as he pointed to the locker rooms. "Your parents can help you get your gear off." He watched Melanie until she got to her mom, and then he looked away.

🐝

"*M*omma, Coach has the schedule for you and practice is next Monday." She got one glove off and was trying to get her helmet off. "It was so much fun. Can we come skating at the rink this weekend? I wanna practice some more."

Jillian unsnapped the straps and helped Melanie take the helmet off. "Sure. Before we leave, I'll check open skate hours." They walked to the locker room. "Put your helmet away and start to get changed."

It was a process undressing Melanie from all the gear, but she was pretty patient for a six-year-old. When it was all off and stowed, she put on her winter coat and boots. Jillian picked up her bag and followed Melanie out to the lobby.

Brett walked to Melanie as Jillian handed her a knit cap.

"Put your hat on and zip your bag."

"Good job today, Melanie." He gave her a big grin.

"Thanks, Coach P." She looked at her mom. "Can I go see if Suzi's still here?"

"Sure, honey. But stay inside."

Melanie skipped away.

Brett's gaze followed her and then swiveled back to Jillian. "She's a good kid."

"She is." She stuck her hands in her pockets. "How did the flowers go over?" She was curious to know who he gave the flowers to, but since he hadn't volunteered the information, it wasn't any of her business. He had committed to every week until the end of the year and steady business was good.

"She loved them." He tilted his head in the direction of the kids. "Where did she learn to skate like that?"

"My mom gave her a pair of skates when she was about three and there was no looking back. For a while, I thought she might want to figure skate, but she doesn't have the patience to learn the spins. She loves speed and quick footwork, which is better suited for hockey." She lifted a shoulder. "So here we are." She glanced around the rink. "Hanging out in the frosty air with cold toes and fingers."

"That does happen. They have warmers for boots and pockets."

"Thanks. I have some. Just in Melanie's excitement, I forgot." She wasn't about to tell Melanie's new coach about her hockey past. She didn't want him to expect more from her daughter than the other kids given that she had been playing pond hockey with Jillian for the last three years.

"Was practice what you thought it would be?"

"More or less." She gave him a small smile. "It's time for us to take off. We still need to have dinner. But see you Monday."

He stepped out of the walkway. "See you next week."

She could feel his eyes follow her as she picked up Melanie's bag. She did check the times for open skate and made a mental note. Sunday morning at nine, they could be on the ice and this time, she'd bring her skates too. It'd feel good to lace up and glide across the smooth surface. She and Melanie could have a race or two. The kid was getting pretty quick.

They walked through the door. "What do you say we stop and get a pizza on the way home to celebrate your first day on a hockey team?"

Melanie's eyes grew round. "Can we have meatballs and extra cheese too?"

"As long as you promise to eat some salad."

A grin filled her daughter's face. "After pizza."

Jillian laughed. "I see where you're going with this negotiation. You won't have room in your belly for veggies once you scarf down a couple of slices. So we'll need to agree you eat salad first and then pizza."

"Okay." She put her hand in Jillian's as they crossed the lot. "How did I do tonight?"

"You were controlled and smooth. Both good qualities of a player but on Sunday, what do you say we do crossovers and unders when you're skating backward. They're tough but something that helps with speed."

"Cool."

Jillian popped the hatch and stowed the bag in the back after she opened the car door. "Hop in and our next stop, the Pizza House."

After Melanie's seat belt clicked, she said, "Momma, how come you don't coach my team? You'd be the best at it."

"Honey"—she looked in her rearview mirror and caught Melanie's eyes—"the only person I want to coach is my favorite girl."

Melanie looked out the window, growing quiet. "Suzi's worried the boys are going to laugh at her, and if you were our coach, you wouldn't let any boy be mean."

She could picture how Melanie's lower lip jutted out when she was being serious. This was definitely a topic that would cause the lip to pout.

"If you think it will be a problem, I can say something to Coach Richards and ask him to keep an eye on things. This way, Suzi won't have to be worried."

"And the boys wouldn't find out, right? I pinkie promised Suzi that you'd know what to do."

If all things in life could be solved with a little conversation and a simple kindness. She was proud of her daughter, doing her best to help a friend.

. . .

*L*ater that night after bath and story time with Melanie, Jillian sat at the kitchen table and worked on her wholesale orders for the upcoming month. She had Heather's wedding flowers to order for the Saturday after Thanksgiving, and planning for holiday centerpieces was easy, along with the construction of wreaths. She needed to order extra ribbon for bows. Especially since she had twenty orders so far. Maybe if she doubled that, she could turn a nice profit, especially since she could forage the evergreens from her parents' farm on the outskirts of town, just as she'd been doing for years now. As usual, they had already volunteered to help her. She could start putting the wreaths together in the days leading up to Black Friday, but maybe people would get in the spirit and buy before the holiday. In looking at her balance sheet, it was clear that a strong end to the year would be vital.

Out of the corner of her eye, she noticed Melanie's hockey bag. Danny always sent the best of everything Melanie needed, but he didn't understand that all she really needed was her dad. Jillian leaned back in the chair and thought of that night seven years ago when she told him they were having a baby. After his jaw had hit the floor and color drained from his face, he promised his financial support but said he wasn't ready to be a hands-on kind of parent. He understood Jillian wanted to have the baby and as long as she didn't have unrealistic expectations for him, they were good.

She could work her butt off providing for her daughter, giving her a good home and someday a college education, but she couldn't provide the one thing Melanie needed: a dad on the sidelines of her life, cheering her on.

Should she reconsider and volunteer to help out as a coach on the team? Maybe if other girls on Melanie's team saw an adult female playing hockey, it would help them gain confidence. It was something to think about, and being around

Brett wouldn't be a hardship, even if he had someone in his life. Looking never hurt anyone, and he was the first guy she had given a second glance to in a long time. Maybe it was time to date again and meeting Brett was a gentle nudge to have her look up and see the possibilities life had to offer.

CHAPTER 4

*B*rett sat across from his mother at the dining room table. Maybe they should have sat at the breakfast bar in the kitchen; there were only two stools in there. The flowers from Jillian's shop were in his dad's place. Funny how he was already thinking of it as *her shop* and not Petals.

"How was your first day of coaching? Were there a lot of kids?" His mother dabbed her lips with a burgundy cloth napkin.

His mom was saving the planet one cloth napkin and linen towel at a time. She always said she was doing her part to help her future grandchildren. At least one of them had hope he'd find someone he'd want to have kids with.

"There were a lot more kids than I thought would turn out for such a small town, but I guess they're coming from the surrounding areas. Some are pretty good; they've played before. I'm going to be working with the younger kids, but there's one little girl, Melanie, who can skate the blades off most of the other kids. Her mom, Jillian, happens to be our new florist."

A glint came into his mom's eye. "Do I detect a note of interest in your voice?"

With a shake of his head, he said, "No. But I do think she taught her daughter to skate or at least supports her passion for the ice. And her equipment is top of the line, which doesn't square with most first-year kids. Why would you invest in expensive equipment when most of it won't fit next year?"

"Maybe they're wealthy and the dad has a good job?"

"I don't think he's in the picture; she doesn't wear a ring, and Melanie never mentioned wanting to tell her dad about practice."

"How do you know that?"

"When I was getting ready to leave last night, I overheard them talking about picking up pizza, and there was no mention of a dad."

"Are you going to see her again?" She stacked the dirty plates and folded her napkin on top.

"We have practice on Monday so I'm sure she'll be there. She's a parent." He wagged a finger in her direction. "Nothing is going to happen, so you can put your Spidey-sense to rest."

"Never say never. It's time you got back out there, even if it's to make some new friends. You need more than your old mother to keep you company." She stood up and picked up the stack of dishes, but Brett leaped up and took them from her.

"You're not old and I love spending time with you and don't worry; I'll make friends. It hasn't been that long since I moved. Especially with coaching, I'll meet people."

She winked. "Like Jillian."

"Mom, I hardly know the woman and I'm her daughter's coach. It's not like we ran into each other and I saved her from a mishap where she fell into my arms and I asked her out on a date like one of your romance novels."

"Books are based on real life; something like that could

happen. You might want to keep your Boy Scout skills sharpened."

"The only thing I plan on sharpening are my skates." He dropped a kiss on her cheek. "The meatloaf was delicious as usual." He leaned against the counter. "Have you given any thought to Thanksgiving in a restaurant? I'm not looking forward to a holiday table without Dad." His eyes drifted to the table and the vase of flowers.

She rinsed off the dinner plates and stacked them in the dishwasher. He knew she was thinking about it, so it could go either way. Patience was the key. He really thought a change of pace was what they both needed. Last Thanksgiving, Dad had been full of life, so cooking a huge meal for just the two of them would be a sharp, sad reminder of what they both had lost.

Mom started the dishwasher and wiped her hands on a towel. "We can go out to eat this year. It'll be a nice change from having to do all the shopping and cooking. With just the two of us, we'd have way too many leftovers." Then her face lit up. "I have a great idea. When I was downtown, I noticed a poster, and they're collecting items for the food bank. I'll give them a donation of a holiday meal in place of cooking."

"That's a great idea, Mom. How did you find out about the food drive?"

"I was on my way to the Library Cat Bookshop, which turned out to be quite charming, when I saw the community billboard. There's going to be a toy drive and an angel tree for area children in need. I'd like to participate in that as well."

This was music to his ears. His mom had a big heart and loved a good cause. "Why don't you see if you can volunteer with sorting or whatever they might need?"

She placed a hand on his arm. "I already did and I'm going out to Gridley's Tree Farm tomorrow. It's where the volunteers are meeting to talk about what needs to be done."

For as long as he could remember, she had never met a stranger.

"That's good news, Mom. I'm going to take off. We'll have reservations for dinner at Antonelli's and I'll stop over Saturday. We can start getting the lights put up outside for Christmas. I know it's early, but it's supposed to be warm out. A good time to get it done."

She dropped her eyes. "I'm not sure if we should."

He placed a hand on her shoulder and she looked at him as a fresh wave of grief washed over him. "We made a promise to Dad to always decorate the house, and I intend to honor his request. Just like I'm going to do with your flowers. And once the decorating is done, I want to take Sunday and dust off my skates and hit the ice. I need some practice."

She arched an eyebrow. "And maybe see the pretty florist and her daughter?"

"Doubtful. I'll see her at practice and then Wednesday for flowers." He pulled on his jacket. "See you Saturday morning, but I'll call tomorrow."

"Brett, you don't need to check on me every day. I'm not some frail, old woman on her last legs. Sixty is the new fifty." A spark glinted in her eyes and then was gone.

"I know, Mom. It's all the change, and I don't want you to be lonely."

Sadness clouded her eyes. "It's part of the process, and we have to grieve to come out the other side." She touched his cheek. "You're a good son, but live your life. I want to see you, of course, and I need you to keep pushing me forward to find my new future."

"I'll talk to you tomorrow, and good luck at the tree farm. I hope you meet some nice people."

"Here. Don't forget the leftovers." She handed him a plastic container and kissed his cheek.

Brett closed the door behind him and stepped into the frosty air. He looked up and drank in the star-filled fall night.

Maybe he should take a page from his mother's book and find a new future. He'd check out the gym near his apartment. So far, he liked living just off Main Street in the small town, but there were times he missed the thrum of working in Boston. He was glad he'd walked to his mom's. He looked at the other houses on the street; they were all similar, some ranch-style or split-level. He was glad his place was on the second floor of an old Victorian. It had a hand-crafted charm that a cookie-cutter place just didn't have.

He strolled down Main Street and past Petals. His eyes were drawn to the second floor. Light spilled from the windows and he wondered if Jillian lived there or did she have a house on the outskirts of town? That question was answered when he saw her tip the blinds without looking down to see who might be on the street. He was glad, since that would have been awkward when he saw her next week, and he wouldn't want her to think he was a creep. He jogged the rest of the way up the street until he turned down Park Street and up the steps to his door.

"*Momma!*" Melanie screamed in the middle of the night.

Jillian leaped out of bed and raced down the hall. She dropped to the bed and slipped her arm around her little girl. "What's the matter, sweetie?"

"I had a bad dream." She snuggled close to Jillian's side. "Can you stay with me for a little while?"

She smoothed the child's wild blond curls. "I'm right here. Do you want to tell me about it?"

She could feel Melanie's head shake and a tiny voice said, "No."

Jillian tucked the covers around her little girl, then stretched her legs out on the bed and leaned against the headboard. "Close your eyes and go back to sleep. Momma's here."

Soon the sound of rhythmic breathing reached her ears. She eased Melanie back on the pillow and placed a kiss on her forehead before going back to her own bed. When she closed her eyes, Brett Parson's face came to mind. His good looks stirred something within her. Was it time to think about dating? Danny wasn't coming back, no matter how much at one time she had wished he would. Mom would be happy to watch Melanie if she wanted to go out, but that would entail getting asked out by someone interesting.

She closed her eyes and drifted off with the thought of a nice guy walking in the park with her and sharing a cup of tea or coffee. She decided to start small. Maybe she'd find out if Brett was single and she'd ask him out. What harm could there be in that? He seemed nice enough.

*J*illian was pouring cereal into Melanie's bowl when she heard little feet clomping down the hall. It sounded like she was wearing a pair of Jillian's high heels.

"Momma"—she came around the corner—"you should wear these pretty red shoes to work today."

On her feet were red three-inch heels with tiny sparkle bows that Jillian had bought for a Halloween party she never went to. Melanie tried to do a pirouette but her feet got tangled up. She went down and giggled. "Don't you think they're nice?"

"They're not work shoes, at least not the kind of work I do in the shop." She watched as Melanie's face fell. "The floors get wet and I might slip."

"But if you worked at the school or something, you could wear them, right?" She broke out in a grin. "You'd be the sparkliest momma of all the other kids."

"Well, since I work with flowers and not in an office, I guess we'll never know. Now, shoes off and bottom on chair. We've got a busy day and we're going to pick up holiday supplies after work to start planning our wreath making."

Melanie grinned. "Can I make one with tiny toys on it again like last year?"

"I was hoping you'd decorate a few. They were in high demand." She added milk and a sprinkle of brown sugar to their oatmeal.

"I had fun at hockey and both coaches were pretty nice, but Coach P was nicest. Did you like him too?"

Jillian sat down at the table and spooned up her oatmeal. "He was very nice. I think it's going to be a good season." But all she could think about were his hazel eyes. She really did need to go on a date and stop thinking about the coach, in spite of wanting to ask him for coffee; for all she knew he had a girlfriend or a wife someplace. After all, the flower order was some kind of indication there was a special woman in his life.

Melanie wiped a splash of milk from the tabletop with her shirt sleeve. "I can't wait until we go skating on Sunday. You're the bestest hockey player ever."

"Sweetie, that was a long time ago. I hung up my skates before you were born."

"I know, but Gram and I have watched your old games, and she says you were like lightning on the ice—fast and lethal." She shrugged. "But I dunno what it means."

Jillian couldn't help but laugh. Mom had always been her biggest fan; it was too bad her career had been cut short. She ran a hand over Melanie's curls. But the life she had now was better than all the medals and trophies in the world.

CHAPTER 5

Sunday was cold and rainy but Melanie was up early, chomping at the bit to get to the rink even though it was Jillian's only day off. Stick time started at ten and they needed to hurry. She made Melanie pancakes and bacon to fuel their time on the ice. Their tote bags were packed with helmets, skates, gloves and hand warmers, water bottles, and some snacks.

Patting her tummy, Melanie grinned. "Good pancakes, Momma. The chocolate chips were the best part."

"Put your plate and fork in the sink and brush your teeth so we can go. I'd like to get there by eight." What she didn't say was she was hoping the ice would be quiet so she could run some old drills with Melanie, but she wouldn't if it was crowded. People in town had finally stopped talking about her missing the Olympics and it was still a tiny regret that all she had worked for didn't materialize. Now women's professional hockey teams were expanding, and if Melanie wanted to live a pro athlete's life, she'd have the opportunity.

"I'm ready!"

Jillian heard a thump, which she guessed was the tote bag falling on the floor.

She dried her hands and walked into the front hall where, just as she suspected, the bag was on the ground and water bottles had rolled across the floor. Melanie looked up and grinned.

"Sorry, Momma. I just needed to add something and, well, it kinda fell over." She continued to stash items back in the bag.

"It's okay, sweetie. No harm done." She tossed in the last few items on the floor and pointed to Melanie's sweatpants. "Put those on and your coat and we'll be ready to go."

"What about your snow pants?" Melanie looked around. "It's cold in there."

"I'm wearing my warm-up suit from college, so I'll be fine." She brushed a curl off Melanie's forehead. Her blue eyes twinkled like Christmas lights. "I was thinking we could stop at the diner for lunch afterward and then drive out to the farm and visit with Gram and Grandpa. You can ask Gram if you can help make pies this year for Thanksgiving."

"Am I gonna stay at Gram's when school is on vacation?"

Jillian held Melanie's bright-pink coat for her to slip her arms in before zipping it up. "That's the plan."

"I have fun when we bake cookies." She picked up the tote, which thumped on each stair as they walked down and out the back door. "I'm strong, right?"

"The strongest girl ever." Jillian pushed the door open. The cold air was a shock after the warmth of the apartment. "Ready to go skate?"

Melanie tilted her head to one side and, squinting into the bright sun, said, "We're gonna skate like the wind, right?"

With a laugh, Jillian said, "After we do some drills, we'll have some real fun."

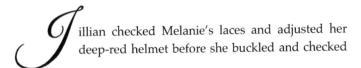 illian checked Melanie's laces and adjusted her deep-red helmet before she buckled and checked

the straps. "Give me a couple of minutes and I'll be ready too."

She finished lacing her skates, zipped her short jacket, and clipped her helmet strap. She noted they had the ice to themselves so far. Apparently, it was too early for families, which made her happy.

She knelt down. "Change of plans. Let's free skate for a bit, and then we'll get down to some footwork. We'll use the lines in the ice instead of the cones you'll use at practice. Does that sound okay?"

Melanie's head bobbed and she grabbed Jillian's hand, barely able to contain her excitement. "Come on, Momma. Let's go."

With a few steps, they were gliding over the ice, using slow and easy strides to warm up. For Jillian, being on the ice was like coming home. It had always been this way, from her first set of double runner blades and Grosvenors Pond. Then her dad had built forms in the side yard and flooded it as soon as it got cold enough to freeze. It was then she discovered hockey, and it was love the first time she held a stick.

Lost in the memory of racing down the ice at full speed, driving the puck into the goal, she took Melanie's hand and tugged her along, slowly increasing their speed. She had been good as a kid, but Melanie had more natural talent as well as the heart to play. They approached the rink wall and Melanie pulled her hand away, did a hard stop and pivot, and then took off at top speed, laughing as she yelled, "Come on, Momma! Race me!"

It was always like this when the ice was virtually empty. Melanie wanted to skate fast.

"Just pay attention and no hot doggin' it." She let Melanie set the pace, oblivious to everything except her daughter. She kept an eagle eye on her in case Melanie lost focus; she could easily fall. But the lower lip jutting out indicated focus was not an issue today. They skated the length of the rink quite a few times before Melanie skidded to a stop. She was beaming.

"That was fun!"

The sound of hands clapping drew Jillian's attention to the sidelines. Brett was standing on the ice, his eyes wide with pleasant surprise. He glided across the ice and stopped in front of them.

"She's going to be a pepper pot, isn't she?"

Melanie took Jillian's hand and slid to her side. She wrinkled her nose. "Pepper makes me sneeze."

With a laugh, Brett knelt down in front of Melanie. "It means you're quick on the ice." He looked up at Jillian. "And it seems your mom is one too."

"Momma has trophies for hockey. They're at Grandma's house in the den."

Now he stood up. "Nice."

She could feel her cheeks flush, and it wasn't from the cold of the ice rink. "It was a long time ago."

"Before I was born. We're gonna do some drills. Wanna see?"

He jammed his hands in his coat pockets. "Do you mind?" He cocked his head to one side.

"It's a public rink." She pushed off in the direction of their bags. This was not what she had expected, to have to explain herself to Brett about her college days. Not that she had anything to be ashamed of, but it was the past. Who was she trying to kid? It was about missing the Olympics and any other opportunities that may have come her way.

*B*rett watched them, Jillian constantly directing and encouraging her daughter. It was obvious to anyone watching this was something they had done many times before—and Jillian definitely knew her stuff. After another ten minutes of moving through the drill, they stopped.

"Water break." Jillian skated over to the bench and grabbed their water bottles and handed one to Melanie.

"The two of you are really good."

Melanie handed the water bottle back and asked if she could go skate. Jillian nodded and took a long drink.

"You should have said you had played before. Why aren't you coaching?" Brett wasn't sure what to say to this woman who was better on her skates than some of the guys he had played with in college.

"It's better for Melanie if she has an unbiased coach." She put the cap on her now-empty bottle and tossed it into her bag. "I'm better as a spectator." Her eyes never left Melanie as she skimmed the ice. "I love watching her skate. It's something that makes her happy."

"Why didn't she join the team before now?"

"I didn't want my past to influence her so I waited until she asked. The last thing she needs is to have a mom who pressured her into playing and fulfill some longing I had." She gave him a brief look. "I want this to be fun for her and for her to learn how to be a part of the team. It will benefit her."

"You're not like some hockey parents I've met. It's refreshing."

"Have you been coaching long?"

"This is my first time; I'm a physical therapist and love the sport. So here I am." He turned away to make room for people coming onto the ice.

When Melanie got to the other end of the ice, Jillian waved and called out, "Time to go."

Melanie turned and was skating backward at a quick speed, then did a one-eighty and all-out raced to Jillian. Her grin showed her pure joy.

"That was fun," she said. "Coach, can you skate backward and do crossunders too?"

"I can. I was a little older than you when I got the hang of it."

She grinned. "Cool."

Jillian gave him an appraising look. "Late bloomer?" Her lips twitched and her eyes held a glint of mischievousness.

"So that's how it's going to be? And how old were you when you mastered it?" He tipped his chin up and narrowed his eyes, smothering his smile.

They skated over to the bench and sat down. "Melanie, we can take our skates off here and dry the blades before we put them in our bag."

Jillian gave him a sidelong look as if trying to decide if she was going to answer him. "Five. I could skate faster backward than forward when I was little."

Melanie looked between the adults. "Momma is faster than lightning."

"I noticed she was pretty quick." He was dying to know where Melanie's dad was. "Does your dad skate like you?"

She shook her head. "I don't know. He lives a long way away and he's so busy with work, he never sees me."

Brett's heart broke for the little girl. He was an adult when he lost his dad; he couldn't imagine what it was like to grow up without one at all. He looked over her head to Jillian and mouthed, *I'm sorry*.

Her face turned to stone. "We're going to take off now." She turned Melanie to the exit. "See you at practice."

Melanie slowed. "Momma, can we ask Coach P to come to the diner with us? Maybe he's hungry too."

"I'm sure he has plans."

Brett wasn't ready to leave them. "If you don't mind, I'm still getting to know the town, so lunch sounds nice."

She chewed on her lower lip. "Do you know where

Dorrit's Diner is on Main Street? It looks like an old railroad car."

"I do, and I can meet you there." He hoped she would agree.

Her smile warmed her eyes. "We'd love to have you join us for lunch. We'll meet you there."

"Great." Hopefully he didn't sound too anxious. This woman was captivating and given the way she could skate, he had to learn more about her past. Now that he knew there wasn't a man in her life, it was even better.

"Your wife or girlfriend is welcome to join us." She gave him a side-glance.

"No girlfriend or wife, just me living in the town of Dickens. Well, my mother lives here too, but that's it."

He could have sworn her smile grew a little wider with that bit of information. After their bags were zipped, he picked them up and they walked out of the rink together. Today was definitely looking up. His mom would be thrilled for him—lunch with a beautiful woman and a sweet little girl.

CHAPTER 6

$\mathscr{T}$en minutes later, Jillian parked in front of Dorrit's. Amy, who ran the place, had an annoying habit of spotting anything different and today, Jillian and Brett having an early lunch would definitely hit her radar. What could she do though? Being rude and uninviting him wasn't an option after Melanie had, and there was no way she was going to scold Melanie for doing what she'd always been taught to do: Be nice. Besides, she had to admit she wanted to get to know him a little better, so this all worked out.

"Isn't it great Coach P is coming with us to lunch? He's really nice."

She glanced in the rearview mirror and saw Melanie waving at Brett as he parked his Jeep next to her. Thankfully he waved back and gave Melanie a smile without looking at Jillian. He got that kids needed sole attention at times, just like adults. A brownie point in his favor.

Melanie climbed over the console and slid out the driver's side door after her mom got out. She held Jillian's hand while they waited on the sidewalk for Brett to join them.

When he reached them, he said, "Thanks again for letting

me tag along. I've wanted to try this place but hate eating out alone."

"You don't have any kids?" Melanie looked up at her mom. "Momma has me so she never has to eat alone."

She ruffled Melanie's blond curls. "That's right, munchkin."

Brett pulled open the door and held it for them. Melanie was running through the options for lunch and at the top of her list was a chocolate milkshake.

When Jillian gave her a sharp look, she said, "Okay. Plain ol' chocolate milk then?"

"That is a good compromise." She placed a hand on Melanie's shoulder and steered her to an empty booth near the front windows, as it happened to be Melanie's favorite table.

Brett trailed behind them, looking around. It was pretty busy, even though it was early for the lunch rush, such as it was in the small town. Church wouldn't be out for at least another half hour, leaf peepers were gone, and it was before the lure of a Dickens Christmas brought in weekenders.

Brett leaned toward her. "Are these mostly locals?"

Melanie slid across the bench seat and Jillian sat next to her, leaving Brett to sit across from them. He clasped his hands on the tabletop and she noticed his long, slender fingers. Her thoughts drifted to how it would feel to have them caress her cheek. Trying to change her train of thought, she looked into his hazel eyes. Today, the gold flecks seemed brighter and she had to stop. "Most people, yes, but there are few unfamiliar faces." She handed him a laminated menu. "After Thanksgiving until January first, this place is off-limits to most of us. The weekend visitor population swells, bringing with it people spending money on gifts, and all businesses get a nice boost."

"Even your flower shop?" He glanced at the menu and set it aside.

"I'll have wreaths that will sell well along with poinsettia plants, but bouquets not as much, and I stay closed on Sundays. It's a family day and the only real day I can devote to Melanie."

She gave her daughter a fond look, but Melanie was oblivious. She flipped over the paper placemat on the table and grabbed a cup of crayons from the table behind them.

"We're going out to Gram and Gramp's farm to scout for bows."

Jillian smiled. "Not bows, boughs." As if she needed to explain further, she said, "I cut the greens from my parents' farm and make the wreaths myself. Melanie decorates a few in her style, with some assistance, and then I do the rest in a more traditional look. It's fun, helps bring in some extra cash, and we get to spend time together."

Why on earth did she just babble on? Brett would probably make an excuse to leave, thinking she might expect him to pay for lunch after the comment about extra cash. She wanted to smack the middle of her forehead but settled for examining the menu as if she had never seen it before.

"That sounds like fun. I've never made a wreath before."

Melanie looked up. "You should come with us and we can show you how."

"Great, and now Melanie is encouraging you to make your own." With a nervous laugh, she looked up to see Amy headed in their direction with a pitcher of water.

"Why, hello there, Melanie, Jillian." She poured three glasses of water and glanced at Brett. "Who's your friend?"

Jillian said, "Amy, this is Brett Parsons. He's Melanie's hockey coach."

"Pleased to meet you, Amy." He shook her hand. "I moved into town a couple of months ago and this is my first time here."

"Welcome, and if you want to know what's good"—she

grinned—"everything." With an exaggerated wink, she said, "I'll be back in a minute to get your order."

Waiting until she was a good distance away and chatting up another table, Jillian leaned across the Formica tabletop. "That's code for she's going to wait on us instead of someone else to see what scoop she can get about you. She's one of our more colorful residents. Wouldn't hurt a fly but loves to be in the information loop."

Brett glanced in Amy's direction. "Thanks for the tip. Now, what really is good?"

Jillian sipped her water. "Amy was right. Everything's good, but my favorite is the cowboy burger and onion rings."

"What's on it?"

"Lettuce, tomato, pepper jack cheese, fried onions, barbeque sauce, and jalapenos on the side." She smacked her lips. "A-mazing."

He gave her an appreciative nod. "You like things spicy?"

Color flushed to his cheeks with the double entendre, which was cute, and then she realized smacking her lips was so unattractive. She really needed to pay attention to sharing a meal with someone other than Melanie or her parents. Not everyone thought it was charming to make funny noises at the table. But this wasn't a date, just acquaintances sharing a simple lunch, more friendly than anything else.

"I do like a little spice in my food, and Melanie's still at the stage where bland is best, so when we're out, I like to indulge."

"I'm having a hot dog and French fries." Melanie didn't bother to look up while she colored.

Amy returned. "What can I get ya, Brett? Jillian and Melanie have a standing order here except today, is it milk or a shake?"

Melanie frowned. "Just chocolate milk."

Brett handed Amy the menu and said with a smile, "I'll

have the same as Jillian." His gaze lingered on her before he turned his attention to Amy.

"I'll get that in and it shouldn't be too long. But you enjoy a relaxing lunch."

※

*B*rett watched the older woman move away from their table. She had the hippie vibe going like she was stuck in the seventies with long, flowing gray hair, a floor-length tie-dyed skirt, hot-pink canvas sneakers, an over-sized sweater, and for an extra dash of flair, a few strands of colorful beads. It was like looking at a picture in a history book and he had no idea anyone still dressed like that as day-to-day attire.

"Do you think I passed the test?" He was still focused on Amy.

"We'll find out when your meal arrives."

He leaned against the booth seat and looked at Jillian, who was stone-faced except for her blue eyes, which were full of laughter. Oh, so she was like that? "Comedienne, huh?"

She lifted one shoulder and casually tossed out, "I do try."

This woman was bewitching. She obviously had a good sense of humor, based on her one- liners, and she was a single mom, a businesswoman. But the skills he'd seen on the ice left him with questions he had to have the answers to.

"Forgive me for being nosy, but where did you play hockey?"

She busied herself with pulling paper napkins from the dispenser on the table. "In college," she said with a modest shrug. "But it's not a big deal."

"Melanie mentioned something about trophies, which tends to tell a different story."

"You know it's a team sport and everyone on the team gets a trophy when they win."

"Momma was captain." Melanie kept coloring her placemat.

The plot thickened and thank goodness someone was sharing a few more details. He cocked an eyebrow. "Where did you go to college?"

"Where did you go?"

"University of Wisconsin. I went on a hockey scholarship."

"Good school. We played against them and for the record, we won." When she lifted her eyes, he could see the pride in them.

His pulse quickened and he swallowed hard. She was fascinating. "Who did you play for?"

"Brown."

In the hockey world, Brown's male and female teams ranked in the top five nationally and when they missed, they never left the top ten. "Good team and school."

"I got a degree in business, and here I am today."

Amy crossed the room with a small tray and three glasses of chocolate milk. He wanted a cola, but then, it was about setting an example for one of his team members, and chocolate milk was a great way to replenish calories burned on the ice.

"Burgers will be done in about five minutes."

Something nudged his memory. Members of the Brown women's team were routinely selected for the women's Olympic teams. Could Jillian have been one of them during her college days? Or was it better to leave it alone and not ask? If she wanted to tell him more, wouldn't she just open up?

"So how did you end up in the flower business?"

She smiled and her eyes softened. "The previous owner was looking to retire when we moved back to town. I had worked there on school breaks through high school and college, so it seemed like a natural fit. I was able to lease the building and business for a few years and then bought both. So now the bank and I are in a long-term partnership."

She didn't sound at all like she had settled; in fact, she really looked happy.

She handed a straw to Melanie and then one to him. "Tell me more about your hockey career. What position did you play?"

"Goalie and I wasn't bad, but I'll confess; I never skated like lightning." He grinned.

She looked at the tabletop. "It's just a family thing; I'm not really that fast and it was a long time ago." She toyed with the straw in her milk. "Where are you living?"

"Park Street just off Main. I'm renting an apartment from the Petersons."

"The house with the purple shutters?"

"The one and only house in all of Dickens with purple shutters, and they just painted the trim a deep burgundy too."

"You can always find your way home."

Melanie tapped on her arm. "When is our lunch coming? Do you think Miss Amy forgot about us?"

Brett looked around to see what he could do to speed things up as Amy walked to them, balancing three plates. She set Melanie's down first and pulled a bottle of ketchup from her side skirt pocket.

"Here you go, Melanie. I had Gus make your fries extra crispy."

She placed the burgers down and gave Jillian a wink. "Enjoy your lunch and holler if you need something else."

Brett looked at his plate and then Jillian's and grinned. "Well, they look the same. Does this mean I can come eat here again?"

She swiped an overdone onion ring off the top of his stack. She crunched down and her eyes twinkled.

"Quality control, and I'd say you're in the clear." She

added a huge dollop of ketchup to her plate and said, "Dig in. You don't want to make her mad when you've come so far in such a short time."

Brett followed suit, dipping the onion rings in the ketchup and taking a big bite of his burger. Jillian did the same. He liked watching her enjoy her burger. A woman who wasn't afraid to eat something messy was rare in his experience, and one he'd have to figure out how to spend more time with. Today had been unexpectedly fun.

"So what do you think? Good, right?"

He pointed to her cheek. "Barbeque sauce." He winked at Melanie. "If we eat our lunch, how about we have ice cream?"

Melanie gave him a long look. "What kind?"

"My favorite is vanilla with rainbow sprinkles."

Her grin split her cheeks. "That's my favorite too!"

He held up his hand and she gave him a high five. "Ice cream buddies. Nice."

CHAPTER 7

$\mathcal{I}$t was Monday again and the third full week of practice. Jillian paused and scanned the rink. Brett was on the ice. His eyes met hers and for a moment, she thought they were letting off enough heat between them to melt the snow on her hat. There were a lot of kids missing and she wondered if it was due to the snow. The drive over had been tough but as a hockey mom, very little deterred her from practice. The late October snow had been predicted for Wednesday, and it had arrived two days ahead of the forecast, but it wouldn't last long; it was just a dusting really.

Brett glided in her direction, a slow and lazy arc around the outside to avoid the kids who were getting their ice legs. His smile widened and the crinkles around his eyes deepened.

He came to a stop in the rink door and crossed to where she was standing. "Hey there. How's it going?" His smile included Melanie. "Ready to hit the ice, Melanie?"

He hadn't waited for Jillian to answer before talking to her daughter, which was nice. He wasn't all about her. Another reason she had begun to like him.

"Hi, Coach P. Momma, I'm gonna go with my friends."

"Just for a few minutes. You need to get dressed." She focused on the man standing in front of her. "Hi, Brett. Looks like there'll be a smaller turnout tonight."

"I'm sure it's the roads. Despite living in New England, not everyone is comfortable driving in snow."

"I guess. I grew up traipsing around in all kinds of weather for games and practice so to me, it's no big deal."

"Me too." He glanced at the kids and then back at her. "I was wondering if you would like to have dinner with me. I had a good time at lunch and I don't know a lot of people in town."

She gave a small laugh. "Are you asking me on a date for lack of friends?"

His faced reddened. "No." And then he relaxed when he saw her grin slide from one side of her face to the other. "You're quite the jokester, but I'd really like to have dinner with you."

She picked Melanie out of the pack. She was laughing with Suzi and their friends. "I'm not sure. It's really busy at night with homework and after I get done in the shop, I'm toast." But she was making excuses; she had been on a few dates when Melanie was younger, but they fizzled out. The guys hadn't seemed to get that she was running a business and raising a daughter and couldn't take off on a whim to do things. But that wasn't what Brett was asking. It was a simple dinner, and she wanted to say yes.

"Would it be easier if we took Melanie with us and did a casual thing?"

That made up her mind. "I'd love to have dinner with you, and I'll ask my mom to watch her. When were you thinking?"

"Saturday? I read about the Holly Hill Inn's holiday kickoff pig roast. I checked the weather. It looks clear but a bit cool. Not at all like tonight."

She had heard about the pig roast for the last few years, always after the fact, and had wanted to go.

"Let me give my mom a call and see if Saturday works. I can let you know after practice." Her heart fluttered in her chest. There wasn't a question in her mind that Mom would jump at the chance to have Melanie at the house, and it would work out since she had been wanting to spend the night at her grandparents' too.

"Okay." He pointed to the ice. "I gotta go, but we'll talk after."

She waved Melanie over to get ready for practice.

*J*illian watched as Melanie took the ice, then pulled out her cell. Mom answered on the second ring.

"You sound like you're in an echo chamber or something," she said.

"Hockey rink." She looked around and it struck her that over twenty years ago, this would have been her mother sitting in a freezer while she practiced.

"I remember those days. I hope you're dressed in layers."

The warmth of Mom's voice calmed her butterflies. "Any chance you can take Melanie overnight Saturday?"

With a soft laugh, she asked, "Do you have a hot date or something?"

She looked across the ice and smiled and watched Brett talking to the kids. "I do."

Without hesitation, she said, "Who's the date with?"

"Brett Parsons, the hockey coach."

"Well, that immediately gives you something in common. And it works out perfectly since we're going to cut greens on Sunday anyway. You can just come out when you get up."

"Thanks. I'll bring her out when I close the shop."

"I'll do you one better. I'll pick her up late Saturday

morning and we can work on crafts for the afternoon, get some bows made for the wreaths, and then Sunday, we can have a few made for sale on Monday. Maybe you can pick up a few sales before Thanksgiving."

"My very own wreathmaking elves." Melanie grinned at her and gave a small wave.

Mom said, "We love making the wreaths every year. You won't let us invest in your business, so it's our way of supporting you."

"You and Dad do enough by watching Melanie during all the school vacations."

"Speaking of being single, tell me about your date. His name doesn't ring a bell."

"He's a transplant. I think he moved here from Boston; his accent leaks out with a few words. He said his mom lives in Dickens and he's a physical therapist along with the part-time coaching gig."

"Maybe one of these days, I'll get to meet him." She paused. "You deserve to have fun, Jillian. I know Danny broke your heart by leaving you when Melanie was born, but that was about him, not you."

She kicked a small piece of paper on the cement floor. "I know, but it hurt. We were having a baby and I gave up my dream of playing hockey in the Olympics for our future. What did he do? Run in the opposite direction to be some tech guy in Silicon Valley. Yeah, financially he supports his daughter, but they're both missing out on so much."

"If you could go back, would you change the past?"

Without hesitation, she said, "No. My daughter is the bright and shining star of my life and I love owning the flower shop." Did she miss playing competitive hockey? Sure, but like all things sports, there was an eventual end to a career. She was lucky enough to find her path earlier in life, and that's what was best for her.

"Alright, well, I'm going to get back to watching practice,

but I'll talk to you tomorrow. Thanks, Mom, for agreeing to take the munchkin."

"Anytime, honey. All you have to do is ask."

"Bye." She stuck the phone back into her jacket pocket and walked over to the Zamboni doors, where she had a good view. She wrapped her fingers around her hand warmers and watched as Brett put the kids through the drills. She was impressed with his patience, considering kids at this age were tough to handle at times.

*a*t the end of practice, Brett kept an eye on Jillian. Melanie was giving her a blow-by-blow about practice like she hadn't been watching.

He skated across the rink and said, "Good job today, Melanie. I like how you help your teammates. It shows you understand the importance of being on a team."

"Thanks, Coach P."

Jillian handed her a bottle of water. She met Brett's eyes over the top of the little girl's head.

"I talked to my mother and Melanie's going to spend time with my parents on Saturday, so if you still want to go out, I'm free."

Melanie wandered away from the adults and was looking at the trophy case.

Brett said, "Great. I'll pick you up at five, if that works. I thought we could get out there early and get a couple of seats by the bonfire."

"Sure, that sounds good."

"Does that give you enough time with work?"

"The shop closes at two, so that will give me time to get organized for Sunday."

His brow wrinkled. "I thought you were closed on Sunday?"

"I am, but we're going to cut greens for my wreaths and start making them."

"That sounds like fun but a lot of work." Jillian was a hard worker, but it must always be that way for a small business owner. Bill, his boss who owned the practice where he worked, spent more time on paperwork than seeing patients on some days.

"I already have ten more orders just this week." She stuck her hands in her coat pockets.

"Ah, right. I think I know of someone who wants two." He was still surprised she didn't just order them and resell. "How does one go about making a wreath?"

"If you're interested, I could save some greens and you can make your own instead of buying them from me."

"I'd like to watch but don't cancel my order, please. I'd hate to make Mom's wreath and have it fall apart while it hangs on the front door. That would be embarrassing."

She dipped her chin and glanced at the floor. "I'm a pretty good teacher and my mom taught me, so you wouldn't have to worry about that."

He thought about it. It would be another reason to get together after Saturday. "Oh, don't say that until you see what I try and cobble together. I got a D in art class."

"The offer stands anytime." She pointed to Melanie and picked up her bag. "We should get changed. Dinner and homework are still on tonight's schedule."

He stepped to one side so she could walk in front of him to the locker room. "See you Wednesday for practice?"

A soft laugh escaped her. "Melanie can't wait for each practice."

"She's enthusiastic."

"I was the same way as a kid. Hockey was my favorite season."

He placed a hand on his chest. "Me too."

She took a step in the direction of the kids. "We should trade sports stories on Saturday."

He relaxed. He could talk hockey all day long. Well, except for the end of his dream.

"Why the frown? We don't have to."

He hadn't realized he did. "No, I got distracted by a work thing. But before we go much further, I have to ask, who's your NHL team?"

She adjusted the shoulder strap on her tote bag. "Are you kidding? I'm from New England so it has to be the Bruins. And for the record, I'm not a fair-weather fan. And you?"

"Maple Leafs, which is kind of New England-ish." He held up his hand. "Wait. There are maple trees in Dickens, so that counts, right?"

She shook her head, a hint of laughter in her voice. "No, not even a little bit. But I'll still have dinner with you despite your lack of loyalty for the home team."

He pretended to stumble back a step. "Thank you. I'd be devastated if my choice of hockey team caused a rift in our new friendship."

"You're safe for now, but you live in Dickens, so you might want to rethink that choice." She bobbed her head toward Melanie. "See you Wednesday."

He watched Melanie slip her hand into Jillian's as they walked over to the locker room. He called out to them, "Have a good night, Jillian."

She turned and walked backward with a smile on her face. "You too, Brett."

With a wave, they went into the locker room. He couldn't wait for Saturday night. There was a lot going on behind her big blue eyes and it was going to be fun learning about her hockey career too.

CHAPTER 8

*D*uring the Saturday morning lull at the flower shop, Jillian's mom came to pick up Melanie. They were going to have a fun time and then tomorrow, Jillian would join them for breakfast at the farm before traipsing in the woods. This week, she had gotten orders for another ten wreaths, so the season was shaping up to be strong.

After they drove away, she thought back over the week. Business had been brisk, with quite a few orders for holiday arrangements, and Brett had been in to pick up his new bouquet. It was still a mystery, but she surmised they were for his mother, which was sweet.

Her phone rang. She needed to pay attention to work and not wonder who was getting the flowers. It didn't really matter.

"Thank you for calling Petals. This is Jillian. How can I brighten your day?"

*T*he next couple of hours went by in a flash and Jillian didn't have time to think about what she was going to wear for her date. But when she finally flipped over

53

the closed sign, she was exhausted. Twenty floral arrangements ordered and to be delivered the day before Thanksgiving and ten more wreath orders. She shot her mom a quick text to see if she could take Melanie next Wednesday too since she'd be busy getting holiday arrangements done, and she'd need Dad to help with deliveries. After hitting send, she shut off the lights, checked the front door, and went up the back stairs.

After pulling up the weather forecast, she scanned the contents of her closet. It was to be a clear and crisp night so she chose a turtleneck sweater in sapphire blue, black jeans, a wool scarf, and a matching hat. Now to get a shower and dressed so she'd be ready for her date with the handsome hockey coach.

*B*rett tucked the tickets in his jacket pocket and ran up the steps to his mom's house. He needed to talk to her about Thanksgiving. They had reservations at Antonelli's for dinner at one o'clock. His family had always had an early dinner on the holiday so they could kick back and relax the rest of the day, watching football.

He rapped on the door as he walked in and called out, "Mom, are you home?"

"In the kitchen." His mom's voice was muffled. He followed the wonderful aroma of cinnamon and ginger; she was baking. Mom's apron was covered with flour as she busily rolled out gingerbread.

"Are you making cookies?"

"I am. There's a bake sale that's raising money for the toy drive at the gazebo tomorrow. You need to stop by and pick up a few things." She gave him a warm smile. "It feels good to be doing something worthwhile."

She looked happy, which made him smile as he swiped a baked gingerbread man and took a bite. "These are good."

She gave him a look up and down. "Where are you off to?"

He sat down at the breakfast bar. "I have a date tonight with Jillian. She owns the florist shop where I buy your flowers. And she's also a mom of one of my kids on the Mites team."

"That's wonderful news. Is she the lady you mentioned a couple weeks ago?"

"She is." He munched the cookie.

"It's about time you started to enjoy life. What are your plans for tonight?"

"We're going to a pig roast at Holly Hill Inn, and there's a bonfire. It should be fun; I've never done something like this. You know, in Boston, these kinds of events aren't every day." He brushed the cookie crumbs off his shirt. "I thought it would be fun and something different than dinner in a restaurant." He gave her a long look. "Speaking of restaurants, are you looking forward to next Thursday?"

She didn't look up from her cookie cutter. "I know you've already made the reservation, and I'm fine with that—on one condition." Her eyebrow arched and she gave him the eye that said what she was about to say was nonnegotiable. "No dessert. I'll make pie for us to have here."

He relaxed and grinned. "Deal." He hopped up and gave her a hug. "You'll see this will be a nice change. And I promise that for Christmas, we'll eat at home."

"Good. Now, what time are you picking up your date?" She filled a tray with more gingerbread men and slid it into the oven.

Brett glanced at his watch. "In about fifteen minutes."

"Then get going, and have a wonderful time." She offered her cheek for a peck. "Dinner tomorrow night?"

"How about I give you a call and maybe we'll do Monday? I have plans tomorrow, but I'll cook for a change."

"Brushing up on your cooking skills just in case you have company sometime?" Mom wiped her hands on a towel, pretending to be noncommittal, but her eyes glinted with mischief. She filled a plate with cookies and covered it with plastic wrap.

He shrugged and laughed. "You never know." He wiped his fingers on the towel to remove the last of the cookie crumbs. "I'll call you in the morning."

She handed him the plate and with a wink, said, "In case you want to share."

⚜

*J*illian arranged her curls under her knit cap and pulled a few tendrils out to frame her face. She added another swish of powder over her cheeks and a smear of bright-pink lipstick. A knock on the door had her taking one final look.

"Coming." She crossed to the top of the stairs and hurried down. The heavy wood door with a stained glass insert swung open. Standing on the step was Brett, holding a plate of gingerbread cookies and with a wide smile that warmed his eyes.

"Hi, Jillian. You look pretty."

"Thank you. Come on upstairs. I just need to shut the lights off and get my coat."

She gave him a once-over, taking in hiking boots, jeans, a dark-green down jacket which complemented his eyes, and a hat and scarf. "You look great too. I checked the weather and the temperature shouldn't get too low tonight, so hopefully we'll be warm enough."

"They're having a bonfire and if we get cold, we can leave.

56

I think the food is served inside or out on picnic tables, so we'll have options."

She thought how nice it would be to cuddle up in front of a fire to stay warm, but she pushed the thought to the recesses of her mind. He followed her up the stairs, still holding the plate of cookies. Was he going to offer them to her? She surmised you didn't bring flowers to a florist and smiled to herself.

When they reached the top of the stairs, they stood in the main living area of the second floor. Brett looked around the open floor plan. His gaze slowly took in the living and kitchen areas in the front to the windows overlooking the street. Jillian and her dad had taken down a few walls. In the back was a hallway leading to the two bedrooms and a bath, with a small laundry area.

He nodded, smiling. "Your place is great. My apartment is all chopped up with smaller rooms but this"—he swept an arm from side to side—"is amazing. Did the place come like this?"

With a laugh, she said, "Hardly. This is what a lot of sweat equity does to an old house. When I bought the building and business, both areas got a full rehab. I wanted Melanie to have space to play. My parents helped me gut both upstairs and down, and then we rebuilt it. Before Dad retired, he was a structural engineer, so he knew how to fix it all."

"I thought you said something about them owning a farm."

"They do; and even though I grew up on it, years ago they leased the land to local farmers. Now Dad has some equipment and putters around, growing trees, but mostly he's just enjoying life."

"Sounds ideal." He handed her the cookie plate. "These are for you. I wasn't sure what to bring a woman who has all the flowers she could want at her disposal, so I thought cookies are a good substitute, and I happen to know they're delicious." He grinned. "My mom makes them every year."

"Thank you. They look good, and Melanie loves ginger-bread men." She set the plate on the large wooden dining table. "Should we go?"

He held her down coat while she slipped into the sleeves. It had been a very long time since a man had done that. It reminded her how a simple gesture could mean so much. She left a single lamp on near the sofa, and the room was bathed in a soft glow from the streetlamp outside her window. It was almost romantic, with the two of them standing side by side with the stars just beyond the glass.

"I'm ready."

Jillian locked the door behind her and inhaled the fresh, crisp air. It was definitely not too cold. She gave Brett a bright smile. "I've never been to a pig roast in November. Have you?"

They walked the short distance to his Jeep. "No, just a summer picnic after college. And for the record, my buddies really were roasting a whole pig on a spit, so I'll guess it might be the same at the inn. At least, I hope so."

He held her door for her and then closed it once she was in. She appreciated the manners. So far, things were going well.

He gave her a sheepish grin and held up his phone. "I have to GPS the address. I'm still learning my way around."

"No worries; I know where we're going. I'll navigate." Jillian chuckled. "I forgot you're not a native, but Holly Hill Inn is just a short drive."

He started the engine and pulled away from the curb. "I'll learn my way around eventually."

"What brought you to Dickens?"

He adjusted the heat and glanced at her. "My parents wanted to retire to a small town away from Boston, and they used to come here for the Christmas Tree lighting every year and stay at the inn. It was then they fell in love with the town. They moved here a little over a year ago but right after, my dad got sick and passed away. It took some time for me to find a job and move here since my mom wanted to stay."

"That's really sweet that you changed your life for your mother."

"Before my dad passed, he asked me to look after her— not that she's elderly. She's actually pretty spunky—but after all they did for me when I was growing up, I thought it was the only thing to do. Mom gave up a lot so I could play hockey, like yours did, I'm sure. Besides, I was tired of living in the city, and small-town life held a certain appeal." He flashed her a smile. "I have a good job, am involved with hockey again, and I'm making some new friends."

She pointed to a sign up ahead. "Turn left and we'll be at the inn in less than five minutes." She folded her hands in her lap, resisting the impulse to place a hand on his arm. "I'm glad you moved to town, and you're right; Dickens is a good place to live, no matter how old or young you are."

CHAPTER 9

$\mathcal{B}$rett and Jillian followed a group of people to the
barn. The inn's parking lot was already overflowing.

"Have you ever been to any events out here?"

"No. I've been to a wedding, but with the shop being open
six days a week, there's not a lot of downtime except holidays, and then I'm usually exhausted from work and using
the time to recover."

He looped his arm through hers, pleased she had made
time for him. "You don't have anyone who works for you?"

"My parents help out and I'm thinking of hiring someone
part-time to handle the front for walk-in sales, but the
thought of expanding before I can financially support
someone else is nerve-racking. What if I screw up and my
business starts to tank and then I've let someone else down?
As it is, I worry about Melanie's financial future." She kicked
the ground. "It's a lot to think about."

"Yeah, I see where you're coming from." He withdrew the
tickets from his jacket and handed them to a man at the barn
door, who in turn handed them each a bright-green plastic
wrist bracelet. "Have a good time and eat lots of food."

"Thank you." Jillian adjusted the bracelet so it could easily be seen.

Brett held out his hand. "Should we wander around and find something to drink?"

She placed her hand in his and he noticed it was cool. "Did you bring gloves?"

"I'll warm up soon."

She gave him a dazzling smile and he tightened his clasp. They skirted the barn and strolled to the bonfire area, which was ringed with Adirondack chairs and couples sitting close to the blaze.

"Do you want to wait here and I'll get us drinks?"

"I'll go with you, and then we'll come back." She took in the view. "It's beautiful out here. The fire creates a wonderful glow." She pointed to a path that was lit with more torches. "Let's walk down to the gazebo first before it gets dark." She glanced in the direction of the barn. "No one is in line yet for dinner."

Changing direction, they walked down a path covered in wood chips. The gazebo was a short distance away from the central gathering area, and carriage lanterns were strategically placed to illuminate its outer edge. Cornstalks and pumpkins decorated the steps. The air was still and the pond reflected the moon rising in the sky.

"I've never seen the gazebo at night." She clasped his hand with hers. "What do you think?"

He was looking at Jillian. "Stunning."

He draped an arm around her shoulders and took a step closer, wanting to kiss her in the warm golden light. She turned to him and her mouth parted slightly, as if inviting him in. He tentatively lowered his lips to her. Her heartbeat ticked up, and then she tipped her head and explored his mouth.

Time slowed and the rest of the world slipped away. She

pulled away, breaking the spell that had woven around them, and gave him a small smile. "You're a good kisser."

He cocked his head to one side. "Thanks, but it was the woman I was kissing that made it amazing."

With arms wrapped around each other, they turned to look across the water. The barn's lights blazed and it seemed more people had arrived.

"We should get back."

His hand trailed down her arm to her hand. It was chilled. "I have an idea." He took his gloves and gave her the left one. He put the right one on, and then he took her hand in his and slipped it into his coat pocket. "Now we can walk back to the barn."

She hugged his arm. "I'm starved."

*B*eing with Brett was easy. But it was unlike her to kiss a guy so fast, especially on the first date. He was sweet and carefree, just like she had seen in practice— well, the easygoing part. The sweet side was really nice. And the gingerbread cookies were a unique touch. With the few dates she had over the last few years, the guy would say he had no idea what to do in place of flowers. It had been a cop-out, but she wouldn't mind flowers. After all, she loved them and even if they came from the market, she'd be thrilled—or heck, pick wildflowers. She took a look around and reminded herself that wasn't an option this time of year. She gave a soft laugh.

"What's so funny?"

He looked into her eyes. The torch light caught the gold flecks in his.

"Just thinking about wildflowers and how while this time of year is good for my business, no one can stop and pick any."

"True. What's your favorite flower?"

"That's a good question. I love them all, but if you'd make me choose just one, I would say a daisy."

"That's an interesting choice. Why is that?"

"I love the meaning of flowers. Take the daisy. Did you know it's a composite flower? That means there are two flowers combined. In the yellow center is what's called a disc floret, and the petals are a ray floret. Because they are the perfect blend of two in one, they symbolize true love. It's why brides often like them in their bouquets. And one final tidbit, the term *fresh as a daisy* comes from the Old English, since the petals fold over the center at night and then open the next day. Hence, fresh as a daisy." She grinned as they approached the barn. "Enough anecdotal talk about flowers. It's showing I'm a little geeky about them."

He squeezed her hand in his coat pocket. "I like that you're passionate about what you do."

She was pleased that he didn't seem to think it was weird that she knew useless trivia about flowers. She should know about the care and how to keep blooms fresh, but Danny had thought her obsession with pretty petals, even back in college, was odd. It just dawned on her that flowers had been a part of her life even then. It was as if she was right where she was meant to be.

She pulled her hand away and Brett had her step in front of him when they entered the barn. It was brightly lit, and strands of white twinkle lights were draped on the walls and beams. Tables were scattered around the open space where groups of people congregated. A long buffet spread was on the other side of the room with a sliding door open to a large space where Jillian could see people cooking.

"Let's go take a look." She pointed to the door. "There looks to be a huge fire on that side too."

He took her hand. "Sure."

They stepped into the back of the small group that had

formed at the doorway and sure enough, a large pig was slowly rotating on a spit, and she also noticed what looked like metal teepees with chickens spinning on string around an open fire. Grease sizzled as it hit the wood coals. The chefs were wearing chaps over their clothes, which must protect them from the heat of the blaze, and another odd-looking piece of metal equipment caught her eye. It had flat shelves, each one loaded with vegetables and potatoes roasting over small fires. The smell made her mouth water and her stomach groan in anticipation.

"Now, this is outdoor cooking." Brett tugged her to the right so they could get a closer look. "I had no idea this event was so elaborate." He gestured to a tall man with a well-trimmed beard. "Think that is the main chef? He seems to be directing the crew like a conductor and his orchestra. This is not their first time working together."

A petite blond woman approached the group. "Welcome, everyone, to our harvest dinner. I'm Amelia. We should be eating shortly, but I'd be happy to answer any questions you might have."

A woman called out, "What's on the menu besides roast pig?"

"The best question of all. Spit-roasted chicken, seasonal fall vegetables, potatoes, and apple crumble cooked over the fire and, of course, my personal favorite, fresh baked bread off the fire."

Brett asked, "You're cooking everything over fire?"

Amelia smiled broadly. "Yes. Everything you'll enjoy this evening will have been prepared right here. All of the food has been sourced locally, within a fifty-mile radius, including the chickens and pigs. The beers and wines are also local. Our goal is to provide the ultimate farm-to-table experience."

He turned to Jillian as he gave a low whistle. "I had no idea it would be such a grand event. I thought it was an ordinary pig roast."

"I'd love to try a local wine or beer. Care to walk to the bar with me?"

"I thought you'd never make the suggestion."

As they approached one of the two bars, she realized they were permanent. They must be turning this part of the inn into an event space. It would make a wonderful setting for all kinds of parties and weddings. She could picture the floral arrangements placed around the room; she could transform it into a garden paradise. She made a mental note to reach out to Amelia to see if they could work together for future events.

"Oh, look over there. It's Vera and Tony. I did the flowers for their wedding last Christmas at the gazebo in the town square."

His brow furrowed. "I was with my parents last Christmas Eve. Is that the wedding you are talking about?"

"Yes. I didn't see you there."

"I wasn't there as a guest. Dad wanted to take a walk and we happened to see the wedding ceremony."

"It was very romantic. They met the year before, when Tony broke down on the way into town and Vera picked him up, only to discover his uncle and her mom were living together."

The bartender gave them their order of seasonal ales.

Jillian placed a hand on his arm. "And they look like they're expanding their family this year."

"Lucky them."

Did she denote a tone of wistfulness in his voice? "Let's claim our table and get some dinner." She wanted to know more about Brett.

After they settled into a table for two with overfull dinner plates and a bowl of crumble and fresh whipped cream, Jillian asked, "Tell me about your hockey career and how you became a physical therapist."

He pulled off a hunk of bread and buttered it. "Not much to tell. I played in college, wanted to go pro, but it wasn't in the cards. So I pivoted and got a dual bachelor's in physical therapist and athletic training. At some point, I want to get my doctorate. I think it might have been the reason I had a tough time getting a job in Dickens. My goal was to work with professional hockey teams as a trainer, but that changed when my dad got sick."

"You were on track for the NHL?"

"Until I ended up with a torn retina. I wasn't going to take the chance of going blind if I got hit wrong in the future, so I unlaced my skates." He looked away from her. "Coaching is the best way for me to stay involved, so when I heard about the need for more coaches with the youth league, I jumped at the chance." He sipped his beer. "What about you? Melanie said you have trophies and I've seen you skate. There's more to your story than playing at the college level, isn't there?"

"I was supposed to go to the Olympics with the women's team but I got pregnant, so dreams changed. Like you said, I had to pivot."

"And her father? He's not in the picture?"

Jillian looked in his eyes. "He financially supports her and prefers it this way." She could hear the bitterness in her voice. "It's better to not force him to be present in her life so she doesn't get disappointed by him."

He placed a hand over hers. "I'm sorry. He's missing out on a great girl." He leaned across the table and tilted her chin up, then placed a tender kiss on her mouth. "She's amazing like her mom."

CHAPTER 10

*B*rett and Jillian held hands as they sat on a bench in front of the roaring bonfire. A guy strummed a guitar and smiled when people began to sing along. This was definitely one of the best first dates she had since Danny. By the look of contentment on Brett's face, she'd say he was having a good time too.

She shivered and he wrapped his arms around her waist and held her close.

"Do you want to head out?" His eyes searched hers.

"Not unless you're ready to leave."

"I thought we'd have a hand pie or two before we left."

"That sounds like a perfect way to wrap up the bonfire." She tucked a stray curl under her knit hat. "And speaking of pie, there's Amelia carrying a tray laden with all the fixings—and the pie irons, too."

She leaned forward and signaled to Amelia, who set a loaded platter on the table next to Brett. "Help yourself; there is plenty more and we have coffee, cocoa, or you can have a hot toddy as a nightcap."

Jillian said, "Hmm, that all sounds good."

He held up his hand. "Do we go inside to order?"

Amelia gave him a friendly smile. "I can get you something to drink. What would you like?"

"Jillian?" he asked.

She didn't have to think twice. "Cocoa, please."

Brett said, "Make that two."

"If you wanted something stronger, don't let me stop you," Jillian said. "I'm kind of a lightweight when it comes to alcohol and tomorrow is going to be busy, so I need to be clearheaded."

"I thought about coffee, but I'm getting to be an old man and too much caffeine will keep me up, but the warm milk and chocolate will mellow me out." He pulled her a little closer. "Are you sure you're not too cold?"

"A good part of my life, and yours too, was spent on the ice. We should be able to stay out here for hours." She bumped into his side and chuckled.

"True, but that was indoors with zero wind, slightly different than tonight, and we were in constant motion on the ice."

"Do you miss it?" She glanced up into his eyes, which were always the window to the truth. What she saw there said it all. He did.

"Not as much as I once did, but yeah, I do. I spent my entire life planning to be on the ice and one bad crash head-first into the goal post changed my life forever. But what's happened is in the past, so all that is left is acceptance."

He took two cast iron pie makers and added the dough and apple filling before handing her one. "What about you?"

"Things were a little different for me. When I was playing, the highest achievement I was shooting for was the Olympics. I knew that would be the end of my hockey career." She leaned forward and stuck the pie iron into the flames. "But I have no regrets." She gave him a sharp look. "I haven't pushed Melanie into playing so that I can relive my glory days."

He held up his hand. "Whoa, where did that come from? I never thought you did, and it is easy to see when she's skating that she loves it. I'm guessing as much if not more than you did at her age."

"Sorry. I'm a little touchy on the subject. When Melanie asked if she could play, out of courtesy, I let her father know. When we spoke about it, he so much as accused me of that."

"Has he changed his mind now?"

She cocked an eyebrow. "You've seen her equipment; he insisted that she have the best. He thinks spending money equates to love."

He nodded. "After I knew you had played, I wondered why you'd buy everything brand new when kids grow fast and equipment is typically handed around."

"Right. They outgrow everything so fast, not just hockey equipment, and other than her skates, which I do want her to have new as she needs them, the rest we could have borrowed or traded or even upcycled."

She really didn't want to talk about Danny, but it was better that Brett knew there was no love lost between her and Melanie's father.

"Does he see her often?"

She turned her pie over to continue cooking it. "Not in four years and he calls every once in a while, but of course birthdays and Christmas, he goes overboard." She pulled the iron from the fire and leaned it against the edge of the pit to check the pie crust dough. It was golden brown but she wanted to cook it a little longer.

"That looks good. Care to cook mine?"

"It requires patience." She handed him her iron. "I'll check it for you though. Hold mine but don't eat it." She popped his open and said, "See the dough is still pasty white? It needs a little more time."

She placed the handle in his hand and was pleasantly

surprised to feel a zing in hers when they touched. Electricity was a very good sign.

He grinned and she got the impression he felt it too.

"Is this like teaching a man to fish?" He got closer and brushed her lips with his.

"Something like that." She kissed him back. "Let me guess. I need to teach you how to fish too?" A flopping sound caught her attention and she discovered his pie had fallen out of the irons and into the fire. She laughed. "How about we share?"

Amelia approached them with two mugs, mounds of whipped cream arched over the edges. "Here you are."

"Thank you. It looks amazing."

Brett took his too. "Do you hold these kinds of events often?"

Was he already thinking of coming back? She sipped her cocoa. It was creamy, delicious, and steaming hot.

"We try to do something every few months. Our next public event will be Valentine's Day, and then a Spring Fling. We hope you'll join us again, so be sure to be on the lookout for details."

Brett gave her a broad smile. "We most certainly will."

Amelia moved away to talk with another couple.

Brett wiped Jillian's cheek with his glove. "Whipped cream." He held it up as proof before he sampled the cocoa. "I'd attend more of these kinds of events. Would you?"

If he was beating around the bush to see if she'd go out with him again, she'd play along.

"If the right event came along and the right person asked, I just might." She sipped her cocoa while she kept her eyes locked on his.

Laughter filled his eyes and he tapped his temple. "Good to know."

*B*rett was ready to ask her to the Valentine's Day event even though it was still three months away. She was fascinating to talk with and he loved her dry sense of humor. Put together with her good looks, he was shocked she didn't have guys lined up waiting to take her out. Who was he kidding? Maybe they were and he just didn't know it.

"About tomorrow."

She didn't respond.

"I know you said you're going to cut greens for the wreaths you need to make. Would you like an extra set of hands?"

She looked into the crackling fire as if she were weighing her response. Was it because she was going to be with her family, she wasn't really having that great of a time, or because she didn't want him to get too close with Melanie, considering he was her coach?

"You're going to get covered in sap and it's not a glamorous job. We're in the woods for hours."

"Are you trying to scare me off so I rescind the offer?"

She tipped her head and considered her response. "Maybe?"

"Well, that's not going to work. It was a sincere offer and I'd like to help if you could use an extra set of hands, but you'll need to teach me how to fish." He winked.

"We're back to fishing." Her eyes sparkled. "That can be arranged." She gave him a crooked smile. "Melanie can show you the ropes."

He liked the way her blue eyes grew round when she laughed.

"What time should I pick you up?"

She cut the pie in half and handed him a piece in a paper napkin. "I'll be driving the delivery van out, so I'll pick you up. This way, the greens will be stowed in the back and make it easier to unload when I get back to the shop." The corners of her mouth turned down.

"Hey, what's that look for?"

"I was just thinking I really need to get on that part-time employee." Then she brightened. "I'll cook dinner one night next week as payment if you'd like."

"I'll look forward to it." He clinked his mug to hers. "I forgot to ask. What time are you picking me up?"

She laughed. "Breakfast is at eight, so about seven thirty if that's not too early."

So much for a slow and easy start to his Sunday. "Breakfast?"

"My mom always makes us stacks of pancakes before we go out. It's kind of become our tradition."

"Then I'll make sure to come hungry." He polished off his pie. "This is good."

"You think that's good, just wait till you get a taste of my grandmother's famous buttermilk pancake recipe."

"That good?"

"Yup." She grinned. "Nothing like 'em." She grew serious. "But if you change your mind, there're no hard feelings. I realize breakfast and spending the morning with my family might not be something you really want to do."

"You can't uninvite me now. I want to help."

"Alright. But don't say you didn't have the option to back out. And sap is hard to get out of your clothes, so wear stuff that doesn't matter if you get sticky."

"Yes, boss lady."

She licked the last of the apple filling off her fingertips. "I like how that sounds. Maybe I should put an ad in the paper and see if anyone applies."

Brett had an idea, but he'd wait to see if Jillian actually did place a help wanted ad. Flowers and his mom went hand in hand. It might be good for them both; it was something worth considering.

She snuggled back into the crook of his arm as they watched the flames dance. "I've had a great time tonight. Thank you for asking me."

"I have too and hopefully we'll have another date soon."

"I'd like that." She looked up into his eyes and smiled. "Who knew a pig roast in November would be this much fun?"

He certainly hadn't. "Indeed."

CHAPTER 11

$\mathcal{T}$he next morning at exactly seven thirty, Jillian pulled up in front of Brett's apartment. She gave a short toot of the horn and then cringed. It was a Sunday and she shouldn't be laying on the horn so early. The bright-purple door opened and he waved from the top step before he jogged over to the van.

He opened the passenger door and smiled. "Morning."

She noticed he had on faded jeans, work boots, and a heavy jacket that was dotted with what looked like old paint splatters. It was perfect for the day.

"Good morning. One last chance to get out of tromping through the woods. Are you sure you want to volunteer?"

He rubbed his hands together and grinned again. "I'm looking forward to it—especially the pancakes to start the day."

She dropped the van into drive and did a smooth three-point turn and headed back to Main Street. On the way to the farm, they passed Dorrit's Diner, buzzing with activity. A few small groups were lingering on the sidewalk.

"Looks like Amy will have a busy morning." She waved to Vera and Tony and Vera's mom, Georgia, and her husband,

Frank, as they passed. "I did the flowers for both of those weddings."

He waved too. "You told me about the one, but I didn't know about the older couple."

"They got married last summer, so two family weddings in one year. But that is where the similarity ended. The brides had very different styles. Georgia was wildflowers and easy-breezy while Vera was much more traditional with roses, greens, and long trailing red velvet ribbons. The brides and grooms were stunning at each event."

He watched while she talked. "You really love what you do."

"To be a part of people's lives through the use of flowers is an honor. New babies, weddings, and even funerals—the flowers are important. My best friend Heather and John Gridley, from the tree farm, are getting married right after Thanksgiving and I'm doing their flowers. It's going to be a beautiful wedding and I'm happy to be a small part of their special day." She adjusted the fan on the heater to high. "You must like flowers since you pick up a bouquet each week."

"I do, but it's more than that." He glanced out the window and then back to her. "I made a promise to my dad before he passed to make sure Mom had fresh flowers every week. It was something he did since their first date. When they were first married and didn't have a lot of money, he'd pick flowers or just buy a single bloom."

"I'll bet she looked forward to them and loved the sentiment behind them. I could deliver them for you and you wouldn't have to pick them up." She flicked on her blinker and slowed the van as she turned onto the road that led out of town.

"I have two reasons for doing the pickup. I usually have dinner with Mom when I deliver the flowers, and now it gives me a reason to see you midweek."

Her heart did a flip as they cruised down the two-lane

road. That was nice to hear but she reminded herself to focus. The distance between houses was getting farther apart and that meant they'd be at her parents' farm pretty soon. "I like that you stop in, but if you ever need a delivery, always know the option is there."

"I won't forget." He looked around. "I haven't been out this way yet. Are there a lot of farms out here?"

"A few. Gridley's Tree Farm isn't far and there's a dairy farm out here too, but mostly the homes are gentlemen farms. You know, people who retire, have a chunk of land, and want to putter around."

"The dream of many, to retire and dig in the dirt." He chuckled. "My parents sort of had that idea, but for them, the small-town life was the way to go, with flower gardens. Sadly, Dad got sick before he could get much planted."

"I'd be happy to help in the spring if you wanted to plant some roses or something." She tipped her head. "I love to garden but living above the store, I don't get the chance, and at the farm, Mom has it under control."

"Thanks. I might just take you up on that. Mom would love looking out her windows and seeing flowers in bloom."

They drove a few more miles before Brett said, "Is there a secret to cutting the evergreens?"

"Don't cut anything brown except for the limb." A slow smile tipped her lips and she laughed. "Don't worry. Stick close to me and I'll show you the ropes."

*B*rett wasn't sure what he had gotten himself into. He wasn't a gardener or woodsman, but if he got to spend the morning with Jillian, that was maple syrup on the pancake for him. But he thought of how their stories were similar in some ways.

She slowed and turned into a gravel drive. "We're here. The house is just around the next bend."

Evergreen trees lined the driveway, every other one closer to the drive so they all had room to grow to their fullest.

As if reading his mind, Jillian said, "Dad had dreams of growing Christmas trees, but they actually take a ton of maintenance, so he moved to harvesting from the trees for wreaths. We've been making them for at least twenty years." She held up a hand. "And be warned, Melanie is very serious about the wreaths that are made and she'll add a couple of her own touches to almost all we make to sell. But Mom lets her make the ones they'll hang here."

"Good to know."

She parked the van next to a restored dark-green Ford pickup truck.

"Wow, that is right out of a Hallmark card."

She dropped the van keys in a cubby on the dash. "Dad will put a wreath on the grill right after Thanksgiving and it'll stay there until January." She took a long look at the truck. "I never thought about it, but it does look like it should be on a Christmas card."

The side door opened and Melanie came racing toward them. She came to a quick stop when she noticed Jillian wasn't alone.

"Hi, Momma. Hi, Coach P." She looked between them, her smile welcoming.

Jillian dropped to one knee and opened her arms. Hugging Melanie tight, she said, "Brett wanted to help us today and I invited him to breakfast too. Does Gram have the griddle sizzling yet?"

She nodded. "There's huge stack in the oven on warm. Gramps said we need enough to feed an army." She squinted an eye as she looked at Brett. "Are you hungry?"

"Starving." He smiled. "I hear you're a good wreath maker."

"Momma says I'm one of the best. Are you?"

"I've never made one before, and this is my first time collecting branches and pine cones too."

She nodded. "It's okay. I'll show you where the best pine cones and holly berries are. We can use those to decorate them. It's easy."

Jillian stood up. "We should eat breakfast before we charge off into the woods and you, little one, need a coat and boots too." She pointed to the house. "Put a wiggle on it."

She turned and skipped into the house.

Brett held out his hand and Jillian took it with a squeeze. "I hope you're not going to regret this. Melanie is now determined to drag you over every inch of the farm in search of the good stuff, as she calls it."

"Well, I do have two wreaths on order and they need to have lots of good stuff on them."

She shook her head. "We don't sell those. They're for family only, Melanie insists." She turned to look out over the farm. "There is something to be said for the simplicity of a wreath. I'm fond of the classic with some red berries and a beautiful bow."

She sounded almost wistful and he wanted to wrap his arms around her and hold her tight, but now wasn't the time. Not with a little girl anxious to have breakfast and show him the ropes. "Any chance we can make some garland for a porch? At my mom's place, it would look good to have some draped along the railing."

"We can do all kinds of things. Where do you get your tree?"

"I have no idea. We didn't live here last year."

"We get ours at Gridley's. They have a hot cocoa stand and sleigh rides and it's a fun time. Is it something your mom would enjoy?"

"I think she would. When it's time, would you and Melanie go with us?"

"I wouldn't want us to intrude."

It would make it easier for him and Mom to shake things up a bit. He said, "It would be fun. Just give it some thought, okay?"

Before she could respond, Melanie yelled, "Momma, Coach P, breakfast."

She tipped her head toward the house. "We should get inside."

He noticed she never committed to Gridley's and tree shopping. But he'd bring it up after Thanksgiving. He didn't want to rush her into something she wasn't ready for, and maybe having Melanie involved in the tradition of Christmas trees was not the right thing to do.

He opened the kitchen door and she stepped into the old-fashioned-looking kitchen, but he noticed it was made to look that way. It had all the modern conveniences, right down to the center island and prep sink.

Melanie grabbed his hand and pulled him into the kitchen. "Gram, Gramps, this is my hockey coach."

"Mr. Morgan, Mrs. Morgan. I'm Brett Parsons and it's a pleasure to meet you both. Thank you for including me for breakfast today."

Jillian's father shook his hand. "Roy, and this is my wife, Jean. We're always happy to meet Jillian's friends."

Did that mean she had a lot of guys she introduced to her parents? He gave her a look.

"Dad, stop. You make it sound like I parade people through here constantly." Color flushed her cheeks and her eyes brightened as she chuckled. "Brett offered to help today, and we all know an extra set of hands is helpful."

He held his up. "Inexperienced, though."

Roy laughed. "Give us five minutes and you'll be a pro. Please have a seat." He gestured to the large oval oak table. "Coffee?"

Roy's friendly nature reminded him of his dad and he

wished he could be here today. He paused. *I'll enjoy this for you, Dad.* He'd like tramping around the woods. "Yes, please. Can I help with anything?"

"No, but the next time you come out, I'll put you to work."

Jean crossed the room and gave him a polite hug. "We're glad you came, and don't mind Roy. He thinks everyone gets his sense of humor."

"Thanks for including me."

Jillian pulled out two chairs and Melanie slid into one and gestured for Brett to take the other.

"Sit next to me, Coach P."

He looked over her head to Jillian and gave her a quick wink. "Maybe you can tell me about your favorite part of the holidays."

She slid her chair closer to him. "When it snows, Momma brings me out here and we get to build snowmen. It's so much fun."

He kept his gaze on her bright-blue eyes. "That is a lot of fun. Have you ever made a snow fort?"

She shook her head. "No, but we can this year now that you're here to show us how." She looked at her mom. "Can we?"

Jillian poured coffee for the adults and then added cocoa to Melanie's mug.

"If we get enough snow, we can." She put the pot back on the warmer and sat on Brett's other side.

It was nice to be enjoying breakfast with the Morgans. His mom would like them, especially Melanie, who was drowning her short stack of pancakes in syrup.

"Brett, tell us how you got into coaching the kids' hockey team. Have you been coaching long?" Jean passed him the plate of bacon.

He selected a couple of extra crispy slices. "This is the first time, but I've been on the ice since I was four."

"Mom, Brett was turning pro for the Maple Leafs when he got hurt and had to retire."

He hadn't told her what team. In fact, he'd deliberately been obtuse about his career.

She gave him an innocent smile. "Internet."

She was checking him out. Now that certainly piqued his interest—and he liked it. "Did you learn anything else about me?"

"Only that you were a goalie." She gave him a saucy wink.

"Well, just FYI, not everyone can skate like the wind." He added syrup to his pancakes.

Melanie was looking between her mom and Brett.

Her lower lip formed a small pout. Her eyes grew wide and her tone soft. "It's okay, Coach P. Momma says it doesn't matter what position you play, but you have to be a good sport and play hard with your team."

He looked at Melanie but his words were for Jillian. "Everyone has strengths and weaknesses, but you're right. It's the team effort in any relationship that counts the most."

Jillian's eyes softened. "Well said."

CHAPTER 12

$\mathcal{L}$ater that day, Brett carried another armload of tree branches to Jillian's outdoor work bench in the back of Petals. It was her goal to get a few wreaths made before she finished for the day.

She came outside carrying a box. "I've got the rings."

He gestured to the stack of greenery. "The van is empty."

Now that she had retrieved the box of rings, he was going to get his first lesson in wreath making. It was really about more time with Jillian, and he wanted to make plans for next weekend because he was more than interested in this smart and funny woman. Spending the day with her only set in cement what his initial reaction had been: smart, hardworking, a great mom, and beautiful inside and out. Jean was bringing Melanie home in about an hour since the van only had two seats, so he was going to make the most of this time with her.

He pretended to push up his sweatshirt sleeves. "I'm ready for my first lesson."

"Are you sure you want to spend the last few hours of your Sunday hanging out here?"

He took the box from her hands and set it aside. Running

his hand down the sleeve of her sweatshirt, he took her hand. "I've had a great day with you and Melanie and if it's okay, I'd like to stay."

He took a step closer and cupped her cheek with his hand before lowering his mouth to hers, brushing her lips tentatively, an unspoken question if she wanted the kiss to deepen. Within seconds, he had his answer. Her mouth softened and their bodies melded together in a deep and sensual kiss. He would have been happy to keep kissing but sadly, she pulled away, just an inch.

"That was nice." Her voice was soft and for his ears only. She searched his eyes. "Any chance you'd like to spend some time together next weekend?"

"Like a date?" He wanted her to say yes, that was exactly what she meant.

Her laughter held a nervous edge. "I guess we could call it that."

"Friday or Saturday? Or maybe both?"

She placed a hand on his chest. "Can I check with Mom to see what night is best for them to watch Melanie?"

"Sure. I'm Mr. Flexible." Especially when it came to another date with this fascinating woman. She made him want things he thought he could live without: a loving relationship and kids. He wanted what his parents had and spending time with Jillian and Melanie, he didn't feel the overwhelming ache of losing his dad. "And if you want, we can do stick skate with Melanie on Sunday and maybe the diner for brunch again. That is if it's okay we all spend time together?"

"Would you mind if we met at the rink and drove our own cars to Dorrit's? I'm not ready for Melanie to think we're..." Her voice trailed off and she lowered her eyes.

"I get it. Single mom with a child needs to make sure the child doesn't get too attached to some guy." He lifted her chin. "We can take this slow but I really like you, Jillian, and I like Melanie, and I'm serious. I had the best day I can remember in a long time."

"That's not it entirely. I want her to see you as a coach and even though we did spend time together today, it wasn't just the three of us like a unit. I have to protect her; she's been neglected by the one man who should do everything in his power to love and protect her."

His blood got hot. How could any father not want to spend time with his child? It was something he couldn't understand. Some of his best childhood memories were when his dad was by his side at school events, games, or family vacations.

"I know that you don't know me that well, but she's a great kid and I'd never do anything to hurt your daughter. You can count on that."

"I appreciate that, but are you sure you can take this slow?" She tapped her gloved finger on his chest. "I don't want any of us having expectations that can't be realized."

"We can take this at your speed. I'm not going anywhere." He gave her one last tender kiss. "Now, about those wreaths."

Jillian and Brett stood side by side with a metal ring in front of them. She handed him a spool of wire and showed him how to secure the boughs of greens, overlapping the bundles of greenery as they went around the metal ring. "This is when the creativity comes in. You're going to take greens and sprigs of berries, whatever you like, and make bundles that we'll secure with more wire as we go around the ring."

She gathered greens of various shades and a sprig of holly berries and held it up. "Take what looks good and, holding it just like this, place it on the ring, wrap the wire around, and do it again, going all the way around the outside. But take your time; it is essential to keep the bundles uniform in size."

She watched as he gathered the first bundle, pleased to see he grasped the concept on the third try.

"Good. Now secure it and keep going."

They worked in silence while she kept an eye on him, pleased as Brett's confidence grew with each bundle. She couldn't help but think about how good it felt to have him working beside her, sharing a tradition she loved. He held up his first one but where there was a gap when the beginning and end came together, she showed him how a smaller bundle could be inserted, and then a final bow.

Beaming, he held up the finished product. "What do you think? Is it one you can sell?"

"Are you kidding?" She gave him a high five and chuckled. "If you need a part-time job, you're hired."

"I know this isn't rocket science, but I'm pretty pleased with the result." He turned it around and looked at the front and the back, grinning. "I won't quit my day job just yet, but I'm not half bad."

"You've got patience, which in my opinion is key. Now, what do you think about making a few smaller ones with just greens for Melanie to decorate when she gets here?" She set aside the one she had finished and placed two more smaller forms in front of them on the bench.

"I can do that." He started the process again and methodically worked around the next two rings until they were done.

A sharp toot of a horn drew Jillian's attention. "They're here."

Brett said, "Look at your stack compared to mine. It looks like I'm slacking."

She laughed. "I've been doing this for years. Give yourself about ten and you'll speed up."

Melanie burst around the corner with Mom right behind

her. She stopped short. "You didn't wait for me?" Her face fell.

He crouched down to her level. "I wanted your mom to teach me before you got here because I wanted to ask for your help." From the bench, Brett pulled the two wreaths he had just finished. "I was wondering if you could show me how to decorate these with a few small toys, and we could deliver them to the community center as a gift."

"The community center? Why?" She gave him a curious look.

Jillian wanted to see how he would handle Melanie's questions. When he glanced at her, she nodded for him to continue.

"My mom is working on a toy drive and I thought it might be nice if they had some decorations. What do you say? Will you help me?"

She nodded and stuffed her gloves in her pockets. "Momma, is it okay?"

"Of course." Her eyes caught Brett's. She was happy to see how easily he had diffused the situation. He had good instincts when it came to kids. "I have a bag on the counter in the back room that has the toys you picked out. Would you go get it?"

"Gram, wanna come with me?"

Mom eased open the back door to the shop and they disappeared inside. When it closed, Jillian said, "I can't believe you turned her frown around so quickly."

"Well, I thought about asking her to help me this morning and it just popped out now. If it's okay, maybe we could take them over after practice tomorrow. I can check to see what time the center closes."

"I think by eight, so we can meet you there."

"Sounds like a plan." The door banged open and Melanie burst through, holding a paper bag triumphantly in the air.

"I'm ready, Coach P."

He looked over Melanie's head and gave Jillian a quizzical look, but she couldn't read his mind.

"If it's okay with your mom and when we're not at hockey, you can call me Brett."

Melanie looked up at her. "Is it okay, Momma?"

"As long as you remember when we're around other kids at practice or a game, you call him Coach P. It shows respect."

"I will." She shook the bag. "Now, each wreath should have a theme. Got any ideas?"

Brett pointed to the bag she still held in her hands. "We should check out what's inside and go from there."

Melanie proceeded to dump the contents onto the workbench and smiled. "Now we can decide."

*B*rett left the wreaths he and Melanie had decorated at Petals. She had a carport of sorts where she was storing the finished wreaths. Melanie was a bright little girl with a keen eye for detail, like how exactly she thought each theme needed one main focal point. She did one with trains and the other with woodland animals and yet each one complemented the other so they could be hung side by side. It was easy to see she had spent a lot of time around the adults in her young life.

He showered and got off most of the sap from the greens, then heated up a plate of leftovers for his dinner. Even though Jillian had asked him to stay, he thought it was best to give mother and daughter some time together. He had been tempted, even though he'd promised they would take things slow.

He kicked back in his recliner with his laptop, dinner, and the football game on in the background. Since Jillian had confessed to looking him up, his curiosity had gone into overdrive. He wanted to see what he could learn about her hockey career and maybe even something about Melanie's dad. Maybe if he had some idea about that situation, he'd know what to do to ease Jillian's fear of a relationship.

With a few quick searches, he found what he was looking for. Jillian Morgan had played center and was the captain of her college team for three years. After graduation, she played on the US Women's World Team, helping to lead them to victory for two years and before she announced her retirement, she had tried out and won a spot on the Olympic team. When Brett checked the dates and thought of Melanie's age, she *had* made the choice to leave the game for the birth of her daughter, not for lack of opportunity. But why hadn't she returned? Surely she could have done both? He clicked a few more links, but after she left the world of hockey, information dried up.

"So who's Melanie's father and why isn't he in the picture?" Brett frowned as he studied the laptop screen. It didn't have the answers he needed, but if he wanted to have a successful relationship with the amazing Jillian, he'd need to find out.

CHAPTER 13

*J*illian waited until practice was over and most of the other families of Melanie's teammates had left before approaching Brett about their plan to take the wreaths to the community center.

"Good practice today." She kept an eye on Melanie, who was getting a drink of water from the fountain.

"It was. Your daughter is a natural-born leader, especially with some of the less coordinated kids on the team. You should be really proud of her."

"I am." She flashed a smile in Melanie's direction. "She's got a tender heart."

"She does. Just look at the way she jumped at the chance to decorate and donate the wreaths. She was more concerned with getting them just right than anything. You're doing a good job with her."

Brett put blade guards on his skates before he tied his sneakers. "Do you want me to follow you home or do you want to meet me at the community center?"

She had already thought about this question. "Come by Petals now and we can head over together."

His smile widened. "Good thing we had a short practice. I'm sure Melanie is getting hungry."

"If you're interested, we could pick up a pizza after and eat at my place." She tipped her head in Melanie's direction. "She asked if we could have dinner and talk about what other businesses in town might need a wreath."

"Pizza sounds good and I'll give some thought to what else we might be able to do. Maybe instead of donating more decorative items, we could make some and sell them to raise money for the toy drive."

This man continued to surprise her. "That's a great idea. I just need to figure out how to explain to Melanie about Santa. I don't want to spoil the magic for her."

He nodded. "She doesn't get any presents from just you?"

She had an idea. "I give her a few gifts from me, but we could say that Santa needs a helping hand sometimes." She used the word *we* like she and Brett were a couple. If he noticed, he didn't react. "She'd want to help then. Last year, we had to leave out a sandwich for Santa since she thought he might be eating too many cookies."

With a laugh, he asked, "Was it one you liked?"

"We made peanut butter and jelly, and he left her a note saying he took it to go but did drink the milk and eat half a cookie."

"I'll bet that made her day."

Melanie was dragging her bag across the wet floor in their direction. Before the munchkin got within hearing range, she said, "You have no idea."

"Hey, Coach P, did you see it when I made my practice goal?"

"I did. You did a good job tonight."

She beamed. "Thanks. Momma says you just gotta focus. When you were a kid, did you make lots of goals?"

Brett picked up her bag and his. "I was the goalie, so it was my job to defend against players like you."

"I don't want to be a goalie. I think that'd be scary."

"It takes steady nerves, but if you keep focused on trying to score, it'll keep the goalie on the tips of their skates for sure."

He pushed open the door to the rink as he carried Melanie's bag. The snow had started and flakes drifted to the pavement. Melanie tipped back her head and let the flakes fall on her tongue.

"Come on, little one; time to get home," Jillian said. "Brett is going to meet us there and we'll deliver the wreaths and have pizza together."

Melanie held up a hand to give him a high five. "Cool." She waited until Jillian opened her car door and got in.

"See you soon, Melanie."

Jillian opened the hatchback and Brett stowed the bag inside.

"So I'll see you in a few minutes?" She wanted to kiss him and glanced around the parking lot to make sure they were alone. She wasn't ready for everyone to know about her and Brett. She threw caution to the wind and claimed his mouth, kissing him for a few blood-humming moments.

"If you kiss me like that again, the snow might turn to rain." He brushed back a blond curl.

She squeezed his hand. "And just for the record, I like veggies on my pizza, but Melanie is a meatball girl."

He gave a sharp nod and a smile. "Noted."

"Oh, and one last thing, professional goalies are a special kind of crazy to be willing to be the target of a slapshot. Forwards are the smart ones." She pecked his lips and grinned. "And you were a goalie. Hmm."

*H*e waited while she got in her car. He was beginning to think he was nuts, but not for playing goalie. He was nuts about her and a six-year-old mini-Jillian. He waved at the vehicle and she tooted her horn. He couldn't wait to see what Melanie thought of the new idea about selling wreaths to raise money.

*B*rett parked his Jeep in front of Petals and approached the door. It burst open, Melanie rushing out from the other side.

"Hi, Brett. Momma said I can help you put the wreaths in your car and she's almost ready. It's almost Thanksgiving, and then we have school vacation." She was beaming. "I get to help Momma make more wreaths on Wednesday. Are you coming over to help too?"

That sounded like a lot of fun but adulting was tough work, literally. He had patients to treat, so no vacation day for him. "I have to work, but maybe I can help out on Friday if you're still making them."

"Okay." Over her shoulder, she called, "Momma, Brett's here."

She appeared from the back and was carrying the two wreaths. "Hi." Her eyes twinkled and her cheeks were a charming shade of pink with a smudge of dirt on one of them.

"Hi there." He wanted to kiss her but held back with a pair of little blue eyes watching their every move.

He took the wreaths from her hands and wiped the smudge from her cheek, his fingers grazing over her chin. "I'll just put these in the Jeep."

"I need to get Melanie's booster seat from my car."

"I'll get it; is it unlocked?"

She gave him a relieved look and exhaled. "That'd be great and it is. We'll be ready to go in just a minute."

Melanie flipped the Open sign to Closed and walked beside him to the Jeep. "Do you think people will like them?"

"I do. They're wonderful, and it was nice of you to want to

give them away." He opened the back and laid the wreaths in the cargo space. "Now let's get your booster so we can roll."

She put her hand in his and he swore his heart melted; she was so trusting and sweet. She skipped next to him, talking about school, then switched subjects to Thanksgiving.

"What's your favorite pie?"

He noticed an envelope under a windshield wiper and pulled it out. It had Jillian's name written on it. He tucked it into his jacket pocket and proceeded to unhook the seat belt. He couldn't help but wonder why someone would leave a note and not just go inside and talk to her.

"Brett, do you like pie?"

"Sorry, kiddo. Got distracted for a second. My favorite is pecan. What's yours?"

"Chocolate with whipped cream."

He was enjoying the simple conversation. When they got back to his vehicle, he placed the booster seat in back and rocked it from side to side to make sure it wouldn't slide while Jillian locked the door.

"I'm ready. Melanie, buckle up, please."

She hopped in the back seat and buckled the belt. Jillian double-checked it and then closed her door. Before she could open the front passenger door, Brett handed her the envelope.

"I found this on your windshield."

She looked at it and then turned it over. It was sealed.

"Did you see anyone out here?"

He shook his head. "No." He watched as the color drained from her face. She must have recognized the handwriting.

"Jill, are you okay?"

She nodded. "Yeah. Give me a second." She looked up and down the street. "It's from Melanie's father. He's in town."

Brett's heart thudded in his chest. He didn't know the story behind her ex but from her wide eyes and thinned lips, he knew it wasn't good news.

illian's heart pounded in her chest. What the heck was Danny doing in Dickens, and why didn't he call instead of leaving a note? He hated the cold and anything to do with the Northeast. She glanced at the back seat and saw that Melanie was singing to herself. Looking at her sweet face calmed her.

Jillian,

I want to talk to you about Melanie and I'd like to see her. I'll be in town for two days. Call my cell phone or I'll come by your place tonight.

We need to talk.

Danny

She folded the single sheet of paper and slid it back into the envelope. Brett was standing close but not invading her privacy.

"Can I have a minute? I need to make a phone call."

He touched her arm. "Sure. I'll call the community center and let them know we're running a little late."

"Okay, I'll be right back."

She walked a short distance away and withdrew her phone from her coat pocket.

"Danny, it's Jillian. I got your message. What do you want?"

"Well, hello to you too, Jillian. It's nice to hear your voice."

She couldn't read his mood. As so often on the phone, he was a master smooth talker, but in person, his face always told the truth.

She had zero patience for his bull.

"What did you want to talk to me about?"

"Can I come over tonight?"

She looked at Brett, who was leaning into Melanie's door and laughing. Her heart constricted. If only Danny had been even half as nice to her as Brett was.

"I'll come to you."

"But I want to see Melanie too."

"I'll agree to meet you tonight." She put extra emphasis on *I'll* and squeezed her eyes shut. Heaven help them all if she lost her temper. Danny never had any patience with what he referred to as her drama queen act. He hated all displays of emotion.

"Alright. Where do you want to meet? I'm staying at the Holly Hill Inn."

Of course he was staying at the best B and B in town.

"We can meet in the lounge. It's the room to the right of the front door. At eight?" That would give her time to get Melanie settled. But she didn't want to ask her parents to come out this way and especially they didn't need to know Danny was in town.

"I'll see you then."

The line clicked off. She took a deep cleansing breath and straightened her shoulders. It helped her to regain her equilibrium and hopefully Brett had meant it when he had asked if he could help.

He looked up as she walked toward the car. He said to Melanie, "We're leaving now." He closed her door. "How did it go?"

"I'm not sure. I hate to ask, but I need a favor. Is there any chance you can hang out at my place while I meet Danny at eight at the Holly Hill Inn? He's in town for two nights and I don't want him coming to the apartment, not until I know what he wants. The last thing I need is to upset or confuse Melanie."

"I can stay as long as you need." He touched her cheek. "Let's go to the center and then order our pizza. I think you could use a distraction."

She gave him a hard hug and blinked away tears. "Thanks for being here."

"I'm right where I want to be."

She rested her head against him and then kissed his cheek. "Me too."

CHAPTER 14

A couple of hours later, Jillian strode into the lobby of the inn and smiled at a few guests before turning to the room where she was to meet Danny. It had been four years since she had laid eyes on him in person. The last time she had seen him, she was holding her toddler in her arms as he walked away from them.

She had no idea what to expect. Would old feelings surface or would he just be someone from her past?

Her eyes adjusted to the soft light and there he was in an armchair, his long legs stretched out, relaxing in front of the fireplace. Next to him on a table was a glass of amber-colored liquid, more than likely bourbon.

She made her way across the spacious room, her footsteps muffled by the plush Oriental rug under her feet.

"Danny." Her voice broke the quiet of the room.

He looked up. His eyes were unreadable. "Jillian, you came."

She could hear a tinge of surprise in his voice. "I said I would."

"And you are a woman of your word. That, I remember."

He gestured to a vacant chair. "I have herbal tea coming for you."

Well, at least he remembered that tiny detail. She unzipped her down jacket and shrugged it off, laying it over her lap as she sat down. The fire was warm but it didn't touch the chill in her bones. What did he want from her now?

He folded his hands together and gave her an assessing look. "Beautiful as always. The last picture you sent of Melanie, I couldn't help but notice she is the spitting image of you. I don't see a trace of me in her."

"She's determined like you." Jillian wanted to throw him a bone.

"No. Again, she gets that from you. I just don't let anyone or anything get in my way."

Her inner radar dinged. He wasn't here purely because he wanted to see Melanie. There was much more at stake.

"Self-focused is the same as determined."

He gave her a small smile. "I noticed you didn't say single-minded."

"Stop with the word games, Danny. You didn't come to Dickens to sit in this inn and chat."

The front desk clerk came in with a small tray that held a teapot, cup, and saucer along with cream, honey, and sugar packets. She placed it on the table next to Jillian and left.

She didn't move to fix the tea but waited for Danny to say something that was actually important.

"I want to exercise my parental rights."

She felt as if the wind had been sucked from her lungs. It wasn't possible he meant it, and what would that do to her sweet little girl?

"What's going on?"

"I want to have a relationship with my daughter." He picked up his glass and sipped his drink.

"Why now? I was willing to work out a visitation schedule that would suit your lifestyle years ago, but you preferred the arrangement we agreed to while you've been conquering the business world."

"Things change." He stared into the fire and avoided her eyes.

"Why the sudden interest in her?"

"I got a promotion in my division. I'm a vice president now. My career is right on track."

She couldn't fathom why he was asking to have a relationship with his child after six years. Granted, he hadn't wanted to be a dad but their last big argument had been when he insisted he wanted to be acknowledged as her father—and then he had walked away.

"I met someone." His eyes slid in her direction. But he looked at her chin and not in her eyes. "Her name is Debra and I'm getting married in the spring."

"Congratulations, I guess, but I don't know what that has to do with," and the words died on her lips. "She wants Melanie, doesn't she?"

He shook his head. "No, not full-time. You're a great mom. We want to start a family in a year or so and we want Melanie to be a bigger part of our lives."

Her mouth dropped open. Stammering, she said, "You want to start your new life and you want Melanie to be involved? After all this time, Melanie has been nothing more than the occasional phone call, checks, and guilt gifts. She hasn't ever laid eyes on you that she remembers. How do you think she'll feel that all of a sudden you want her around to be a father to her? Do you think that you can create the perfect family now just because you want it?"

"Jillian, keep your voice down." He kept his voice monotone, which infuriated her even more.

She hit the side of the armchair and Danny jumped. "I don't care if people look. I won't allow you to use Melanie as a prop in your new life."

He leaned forward. "I've set up an irrevocable trust fund for her. She'll want for nothing."

"Is that what you think? Money and now your interest will take care of the past neglect?" She got to her feet. The tea cup turned over. "I will not allow you to use a sweet, innocent little girl to score points with your new wife."

"Be reasonable. What are you hoping? That someday you'll meet a guy who'll adopt her?"

"That's not how this works. You don't get to ask questions about how I live my life, or my future." She turned her back to him and then swung around. "I would encourage you to pick up the phone and call your fiancée to tell her my daughter will not add window dressing to your life. When you walked away from us, it broke my heart. I loved you." She dropped her head but unlike Danny, she had to put her daughter first. "If you still want to see Melanie while you're in town, I'll agree to a supervised visit with the three of us together."

He hung his head and in that moment she almost, almost felt sorry for him. Danny had made his choice a long time ago.

"Melanie," Jillian continued, "deserves both of us to be the best we can for her. I can accept you haven't wanted to be in her life, but at least you've supported her financially and she's wanted for nothing. I wish it hadn't taken your fiancée to urge you to get involved with her and that you had discovered for yourself what a terrific human being she is."

"You've done an amazing job with her and with keeping me in the loop, sending copies of her report cards and the occasional picture. I don't deserve it."

Her heart didn't soften. He had looked at what she emailed; she had to concede he wasn't just a signature on a check or fancy gifts on birthdays and at Christmas. Not that Jillian really understood why he didn't want to be in her daughter's life, but she couldn't change that. Not when she got pregnant, and not now. But she could protect Melanie from feeling abandoned by him.

"You're right. You don't. I loved you once, enough to have a baby. Do the right thing for everyone. Melanie can't be included and then excluded in your life when it's inconvenient. It would scar her forever and that's something you'd have to live with." She turned to walk away and then stopped. "Why did you leave the note on my car and not call?"

"I wanted to put you in the driver's seat. If you didn't want to talk to me, you didn't have to call me back."

"That makes no sense, but whatever."

Danny didn't look up or try to stop her as she left the inn. She was shaking as she made her way to the car, and it wasn't from the cold. Hot tears streamed down her face. How could she protect Melanie from knowing her father was rejecting her again? She got in and slammed the door, gripping the steering wheel. Sobs racked her body. He had done it again, shattered her heart with his thoughtless words.

She sat in the car for a long time until her cell pinged. She looked at the incoming text. It was from Brett. *Are you okay?*

She texted back, *On my way home. See you in fifteen.*

He sent her a thumbs-up emoji.

She started the car and pulled her jacket on. She decided if Brett was willing to be a sounding board, she'd talk this out with him when she got home. Her parents had lived through Danny rejecting her and Melanie once. She didn't want them to have to do it again if she could help it. And this was worse, since it was all about putting on a good front for his soon-to-be new wife.

*J*illian slipped off her leather boots and climbed the steps with a heavy heart. The door swung open at the top of the stairs and Brett was there with open arms. She was grateful when he pulled her to his side.

"Rough conversation?"

"Yeah. He knows how to come up with the most self-centered ideas." She stepped out of his comforting embrace and hung up her coat. "Tea?"

"I'll make it. You sit down."

She liked how he jumped in and helped soothe her hurt even if he didn't know what it was. She pointed to where the teabags were and got down two mugs.

"I read Melanie three books before she finally settled in. She seemed to like the idea of prolonging bedtime."

With a small smile, Jillian said, "She knows on a school night, it's two stories. Next time, don't let her wheedle out a third."

"Good to know."

"How did it go, talking about the toy drive?"

"I think she's pretty excited to help out."

"Good." The kettle whistled. Soon the tea was steeping and they sat on the sofa. He was waiting for her to talk, but she didn't feel pressured. She dunked the tea bag several times. The mug warmed her icy hands.

"He wants to have a relationship with her, be a father. And he mentioned he set up an irrevocable trust fund for her."

Brett's mouth hung open. "After all this time?"

She shook her head. "He's getting married next year and they want to have a family and his future wife is encouraging him to include Melanie in their new life."

"What did you tell him?"

"As angry as I was and am at him, I understand, but he can't waffle. He's either in her life or he's not. And looking down the road, how do we handle summer vacations and holidays? They live three thousand miles away. I'm not putting my daughter on a plane by herself so she can fly out there to see him."

He sunk into the cushions. "Wow."

"I know none of this will be resolved tonight, but all these thoughts are rushing around in my head." She nodded. "I still find it shocking that he wants to be involved after all this time."

"What do you think he'll do?" He put an arm around her shoulders and slid closer to her.

"I hope for my daughter's sake, he doesn't break her heart." Fresh tears sprang to her eyes. "I can't believe he thinks he can just show up and everything is all gingerbread and cocoa."

He gave her a warm, one-armed hug. "I'm so very sorry, Jillian."

She let his presence surround her. Nothing could get much worse than this with Danny, and she only hoped it would get better.

She kissed his cheek. "I'm glad you're here."

CHAPTER 15

*T*he next morning, Jillian had a fresh outlook for what lay ahead. She might not be able to sway Danny, but she had options when it came to visitation, and she was determined to do her best to shield Melanie from a potential game. She looked at her phone and noticed a text message from him.

Sorry about last night. You're right. I was being thoughtless. Can I see my daughter before I leave town? I promise not to be a jerk.

She noticed the time stamp. It had come while she was in the shower.

When and where? We'll meet you.

Before she could put the phone down, she got a new text.

Ice cream after school?

Meet you at Dorrit's Diner at four.

She put her phone aside and called down the hall for Melanie to put a wiggle on it. The table had bowls of oatmeal and berries waiting when Melanie sashayed into the room.

"Momma. I'm Ariel today." She twirled around. She was wearing her mermaid princess costume from Halloween, from the long red wig right down to her bare feet in place of fins.

"Good morning, your royalness. Would you care to have breakfast with a simple commoner?"

She giggled. "Momma, you're the queen because I'm the princess." She slipped into her chair and flipped the long red braid over her shoulder.

"Well, this queen needs you to eat your breakfast so I can drop you at school." She decided not to tell Melanie about seeing Danny, just in case he changed his mind. "Your lunch is packed and milk money is inside the bag too."

"When Brett babysat me last night, he asked if I'd help him with a special project."

"He did? And what is that?"

Melanie popped a few berries in her mouth. "Do you know there are some kids who don't get mommy presents on Christmas?"

"Chew with your mouth closed, please, and then you can talk. I know some people do struggle to provide for their children."

Melanie swallowed and then even opened her mouth to show it was empty before she continued. "Well, Brett said there's a toy drive and people can drop off new toys, and then if someone needs a momma toy, they can pick something out. It's kinda like helping Santa deliver presents."

She continued to eat her oatmeal. "Brett said that we could make some wreaths to sell to raise money to buy toys. Brett said it's nice to help people when they need it."

Jillian couldn't help but notice she used the phrase *Brett said* several times. It was cute.

"And where could we sell these wreaths? I'm assuming we've made them in our store?"

She nodded. "Yup, Brett said"—she grinned—"we could sell them at hockey practice next week, but after he gets permission."

"He did, did he? And will he help us make the wreaths we're going to sell?"

Melanie scraped the bottom of her bowl. "Yup, and he said he was going to ask his mom too. She needs a project." She tilted her head. "Why does a momma need a project?"

This was more than she was ready to tackle first thing in the morning, but she did love the idea of getting Melanie involved in helping the community. You could never start kids too young. She remembered as a kid making treat cups for senior citizens who lived in nursing homes, and at Christmas, her Girl Scout troop would go caroling at the hospital too. It always brought a smile to a lot of wrinkled faces.

"It's a fantastic idea and before you go and brush your teeth, call Gram and see if she wants to help too. The more hands we have working together, the more money we can raise."

"Can I go shopping for the toys too?"

There was no way Jillian could resist that sweet face with a smear of oatmeal on her chin. She wiped it with a paper napkin. "Absolutely. We need your expertise in toy selection." She tweaked Melanie's nose. "Call Gram—my phone's on the counter—and then brush your teeth and don't forget to change into school clothes."

She tidied the kitchen while Melanie talked to her mom.

"Here she is, Gram. Bye." She handed Jillian the phone. "She wants to talk to you." She skipped through the living room, singing a song from the mermaid movie without a care in the world.

"Hey, Mom."

"Morning, Jillian. What's this about making wreaths to sell and buy toys?"

"Brett watched Melanie for me last night and while I was out, they talked about the idea. I think it's never too early to learn how to help others."

"I didn't know you needed a sitter; you could have called."

She dropped her voice. "I can't fully explain right now but Danny's in town and I had to see him. If you want, stop in at the shop and I'll fill you in."

"I'll be there by nine."

She smiled into the phone. Mom to the rescue. "Bring coffee and a pastry, please."

"Bye, Jilly, and don't worry. Everything will be fine. Whatever Danny's up to, Dad and I will support you."

It had been just like that from the moment she had told them she was raising a baby as a single woman. Helping but not smothering was their motto. They stepped into their roles as grandparents with ease and in the early months, it was hard to balance a new baby and opening the shop, but that's where living in a small town had its advantages. Customers didn't mind that there was a baby in the shop even when she was fussy. Thankfully Melanie had been an easy baby and she went to daycare when she got a little older, leaving Jillian to focus on being a businesswoman from eight to four.

"Ta-da."

She had been so absorbed in the past, she hadn't heard Melanie come in the room. She was dressed in bright-purple leggings and a long fleece top, with sneakers.

"Now the princess looks ready for school." She knelt down to hug her daughter close.

Melanie squirmed out of her arms. "Momma, you were holding me super tight like you do when I wake up when the monster dream comes. Did you have a bad dream?"

"No. I just love squeezing you because you're my favorite daughter."

"Silly, I'm the only one."

"I know you are." Jillian took a long look at her precious child and gave a silent prayer that nothing would take that sunny smile away from her today. "Ready for school?"

"Ready, Momma."

*J*illian's mom was perched on a stool next to the counter, sipping coffee as she learned what had taken place the previous night.

"Danny asked you to let him spend more time with his daughter—I'm assuming on the West Coast. Is that something he can do?"

"I have no idea, but he was quick to say he set up a trust fund. Like money is what matters to a little girl."

"Someday that little girl will need a college education, and money would certainly help with that."

"Mom, I know college is expensive and I'm trying to save money to build our house on the land you and Dad gave me so things are tight, but I'll still be able to give her an education. And I have a few years too." She held up a hand as her mom opened her mouth. "No, I don't need your money. We're fine. The land is more than generous."

"We want you and our granddaughter to have a home with plenty of land around you. Besides, who else is there to help if we can't help our only child?"

She placed her hand over Mom's. "I appreciate it, but to get back to the Danny situation, he's asked for us to meet him for ice cream at Dorrit's. I'm hoping this means he's had a change of heart. But if he starts to say anything that will hurt her in any way, we're out of there."

"Good." She tossed the paper cup in the trash barrel. "Looks like you've got orders stacked pretty high. Need a hand?"

"I'd love it. I've decided I'm going to advertise for part-time help, a person to handle the front while I create arrangements and work on the website. I want to grow the business, so it's the next step to financial freedom."

"I'm always happy to lend a hand. All you have to do is ask." Mom took the small clipboard with the stack of orders and began to line up vases according to the schedule.

"I appreciate the offer, but I like to keep you on reserve for when I really need help." She grinned. "Like today. In fact, I was going to see if Dad could do some extra deliveries for me this afternoon."

"He's just waiting for your call. He loves doing holiday deliveries." She pointed to the phone. "Call him and then call the paper and get the ad in for the weekend. Strike before the flowers wilt."

"The saying is strike while the iron's hot." Jillian shook her head.

"You're in the flower business, not the laundry business, so I changed it up." She gave a funny little smile and a one-shouldered shrug. "It's called being creative."

"You know, since I'm going to put an ad in the paper, maybe I'll make up a sign for the window too. Who knows; maybe someone will see it and apply in person. I'd rather get the first impression up close instead of over the phone or via email."

"I'll get started and you take care of business." Mom put on a dark-green logo apron and grabbed floral shears. "I'll start with the small arrangements and when you are done, you can go for the larger ones."

Jillian rolled back on her heels and watched as her mother dove into the orders with gusto. There really wasn't anything she wouldn't do to help.

A half hour later, there was a sign in the front window and she was about to call about placing an ad in the Sunday paper, *The Dickens Times*. Before she could get started, a woman about her mom's age entered the shop.

"Good morning. I noticed your sign in the window; you're looking for part-time help. Do you need to hire someone with skills in floral arranging or is a love of all flowers a good starting point?"

She crossed the room and held out her hand. "I'm Jillian Morgan and this is my shop."

"It's a pleasure to meet you. I'm Alice and I'd like to apply for the job—unless, of course, I need special skills."

There was something about this woman that Jillian took an instant liking to. She was warm and personable and she had a nice smile that filled her hazel eyes.

"I'm looking for someone to run the front counter, to wait on customers when they come in, take phone orders, and basically help out as needed."

"I can certainly do all of that."

Jillian's mom came out of the back. "I thought I heard you talking to someone." She smiled. "Alice, what are you doing here?"

"Jean, this is a surprise. Do you work here too?"

"No, this is my daughter Jillian, and I help out from time to time."

Jillian looked between the two women. "I take it you know each other."

Alice said, "We met at Gridley's Tree Farm when I volunteered for the toy drive."

Her mom said, "I'll just go in the back and you can finish talking, but it was nice to see you, Alice, and I'll see you at the meeting next week."

"Take care, Jean."

Jillian looked at her mother's retreating back. "Would you excuse me for just one minute?"

"Of course. Take your time; I'll just enjoy smelling all the flowers."

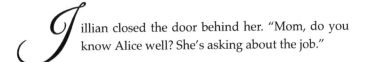

illian closed the door behind her. "Mom, do you know Alice well? She's asking about the job."

"You should hire her. She lost her husband a while back and is at loose ends. She's done amazing things already organizing the toy drive; she jumped right in and rolled up her sleeves."

Jillian looked at the door and made up her mind. "I'm going to do it."

She walked into the front of the shop. "Alice, how does a trial period sound and if we both agree in a month that it's working, we can talk about a small raise."

The other woman's hazel eyes brightened. "When do I start?"

CHAPTER 16

*B*rett was going to surprise Jillian with coffee when he remembered she was meeting her ex with Melanie for ice cream. Instead, he swung by his mom's house. He could hear Christmas music before he even opened the back door, which put a smile on his face.

He stepped into the kitchen and discovered his mom was stirring up what looked like a batch of chocolate chip cookies.

"Hey, what's the occasion?" He scooped out a fingerful and popped it in his mouth. "Good stuff."

She swatted his arm. "Are you ever going to stop eating raw dough?"

"Probably not." He perched on a stool at the island. "What's gotten into you today?"

"I got a part-time job." She radiated happiness. "Can you believe it? I wasn't even trying. I was walking down Main Street, window shopping, and as I was passing a shop, the owner put a sign in the window for help. I walked in and by happy coincidence, I knew the lady's mother. We met at the toy drive and before I knew it, she was asking me to start tomorrow. The holidays are pretty busy for her."

"That's great news. What kind of shop is it?"

"Another happy coincidence. It's the place where you've been buying my flowers, Petals."

He was surprised. "Jillian hired you?"

"She did, and I didn't have to go through a big interview process. We talked, and that was that." She glanced at him. "How well do you know her?"

"Well, I'm her daughter's hockey coach and she's the woman I have started to date."

"Interesting." She began to drop mounds of cookie dough on sheets. "I'm going to take some cookies in with me tomorrow. Sort of a thank you for giving me a chance."

"Does she know we're related?" And the other unasked question was if she would be upset knowing she had just hired his mother when they were starting to get serious. Things were getting complicated.

She looked off in the distance. "I don't know. We started talking, and then Jean came out of the back and less than ten minutes later, I was hired. I would guess she had something to do with it."

"Well, no matter how you got the job, I think cookies will be a nice touch and every day seems to be busy in the shop, so they'll be a good energy boost."

"Who doesn't love homemade chocolate chip cookies?" She slid two trays into the oven. "Now, tell me. What do I owe the happy surprise of you stopping by, and do you want to stay for dinner?"

"Change of plans. I was headed over to Petals before practice to bring Jillian a coffee and detoured here first after remembering we canceled it."

"I don't remember your teams ever taking any time off except for the holiday."

He shrugged. "I don't make the schedule; I just follow it. And dinner sounds good if I can help."

"I'll go one better. You can cook for me and I'll finish the cookies."

"You're on." He washed his hands and couldn't help but wonder how things were going for Jillian. "Potluck it is."

*J*illian sat Melanie on a stool in the back room after she locked the door to Petals on the dot of four.

"I wanted to talk to you before we go to Dorrit's."

Melanie's deep blue eyes widened. "Are we having dinner? I haven't seen Miss Amy in forever."

"We're not having dinner, but we are going to have an ice cream."

She gave Jillian a cautious look. "Dessert before dinner. That isn't allowed."

"On rare occasions we can, and today is going to be one of those times." With a smile, she said, "Your father is in town and he's going to meet us there." She wasn't sure how Melanie would react or if she would even remember what he looked like. It had been over four years since he last breezed through town.

"Are you going to have ice cream too?" But there was no reaction to seeing Danny.

"Yes, I'm thinking I'll order a small hot fudge sundae." Melanie perked up at the mention of a sundae. Better to get her mind on something simple.

"Is Brett coming too?"

That question caught Jillian off guard and it went to show that Melanie had accepted him into their little circle.

"No, it's just the three of us."

Her face fell a little. "Maybe next time he can come with us."

"We can do that." She helped her down and said, "Run upstairs and drop your book bag in the living room so we can go."

"I need to go to the bathroom too."

"Wash your hands, munchkin."

Melanie went out the back door and up the stairs. That went easier than Jillian had thought, even though ice cream before dinner came as a surprise to her, but she took the *rare occasions* comment in stride. She wiped her damp palms on her jeans and shrugged into her jacket. A lead weight sat in her stomach. If there was any chance of Danny saying something to manipulate Melanie with promises of heaven only knew what, there would be hell to pay.

Little feet pounded down the stairs with Melanie calling to her, "I'm ready."

Jillian slung her bag over her shoulder and, with keys and phone in hand, pasted a bright smile on her face. In an hour, this would be behind both of them. She hoped.

*M*elanie held tight to her hand as they crossed the street. Dorrit's was a few steps away when Melanie stopped.

"Momma, is my father going to be here for Thanksgiving?"

Jillian knelt down and placed her hand on a rosy cheek. "I don't think so. This is a quick trip for him. Maybe next time, he'll stay longer." Should she have even introduced the idea of another trip? She'd cross that bridge when she came to it.

"Can I ask him?"

"I'll tell you what. I'll ask him what his plans are, okay?"

She gave a brisk nod and grinned. "I'm gonna have vanilla ice cream with rainbow sprinkles."

Jillian relaxed. She was going to take a page from her daughter's playbook and keep it simple and breezy. "Do you think I should have strawberry with chocolate sprinkles or a sundae?"

"The sundae, and can I have a bite?"

"Don't you always have a spoonful or two?"

Melanie skipped the last few steps to the door. She could see Danny inside, sitting at a table near the back but in front of a window. He held up his hand in greeting but his eyes were glued to Melanie. A smile slipped over his face.

She gripped Jillian's hand tighter.

"It's okay, honey. That's your dad."

Her lower lip quivered. "Do you think he'll like me?"

Giving a quick squeeze to her hand, Jillian said, "What's not to like?"

Danny rose from the table and his eyes grew brighter. "Hi, Melanie. My goodness, you have gotten so big."

"Hi." Her voice came out as a whisper and she half hid behind her mom.

If he noticed she didn't call him dad, he didn't show it.

"I'm glad you could come for ice cream. I've been looking forward to seeing you."

She looked up at the man who towered over her. His dark hair was short and straight and his pale-blue eyes were not as deep as Melanie's.

"You were?"

"Yes. Let's sit down."

Melanie and Jillian sat in chairs across from Danny. Since they had walked in, he hadn't stopped smiling.

Amy came over and took their ice cream order and promised to be back in a few minutes. She had given Danny a long look, but there was no chitchat this time and her expression was unreadable.

"Your mom said you're having fun at hockey."

"It's the best and I got the nicest skates, and you should see my gear bag. It's so cool."

He didn't seem to be annoyed she didn't realize he had bought her equipment.

"How's school going? Do you have a favorite subject?"

Amy returned with three dishes of ice cream, and Jillian waited for Melanie to dip her spoon into her dish first.

"She gets the first bite." As if she needed to explain further, Jillian said, "It's something my mom started with me and I carried it forward."

Danny slid his cup closer to Melanie. "Do you want to try my ice cream? It's rocky road."

She looked at Jillian. "Can I, Momma?"

"Sure." Her eyes met Danny's. What was going on? They were acting like they were some kind of family unit, which they weren't. Danny had always made that very clear.

"Hmm, that's okay, but I like vanilla and rainbow sprinkles best." She turned her attention to her dish of vanilla. "You can taste mine if you want."

"Why, thank you." He dipped his spoon in the dish and seemed to enjoy the simple pleasure of sharing.

"So how is school, Melanie?"

"It's good. I like art, gym, and reading the best." She attacked her ice cream with gusto and a drip slipped down her chin.

Jillian swirled the sprinkles into her whipped cream, waiting for Danny to say something. Her patience was stretched thin when he finally cleared his throat.

"I thought about what you said." His eyes slid to Melanie and then back to her. "Debra and I had a long talk and things are good back home, but I still need to figure a few things out."

Jillian gave him a long, hard look. She didn't give a flying fig about his relationship with his fiancée. What she wanted to know was what he planned to do about his daughter. Which, given the present circumstance, she couldn't ask him.

"Good to know."

"What I said the other night?" He waited until she looked up. "I meant it. I want to have a more active role."

What did that mean? Like he wanted visitation? There was no freaking way she would send her little girl off to stay with strangers.

He must have recognized the look on her face as the same as if her feet were drying in cement.

"Jillian, it'll be a very slow process. Please don't worry. I wouldn't do anything to cause waves. I'd like to start with weekly phone calls if that's okay, and maybe this summer come back to Dickens and stay for a few days, maybe a week so we can do day trips. But only if we're at that point."

She watched Melanie savoring her ice cream. The last thing Jillian wanted was to deprive her daughter of her biological father. Even though she had hated Danny when he decided to walk away from them, at one time, he had been the man she had loved. If nothing else, she needed to do this for Melanie.

"We can start slow and see how things evolve, but if at any time I feel that things are moving too fast, all bets are off. It takes more to be considered in that role—" She didn't want to use the word *parent* to avoid Melanie catching wind of something. "I'm sure you understand."

"Absolutely. All I ask is the opportunity, and I'd like to set up a computer for her so we could do FaceTime calls so we can see each other. Would that be okay?"

"That can happen with my tablet. No need to buy something new."

"Momma, can I go wash my hands in Miss Amy's special sink?" She held up her sticky fingers.

Jillian said, "Please ask Miss Amy before you go behind the counter."

"I will." She crossed the room while her mother and father watched her.

"She's amazing." Danny's voice was soft and filled with wonder.

"Melanie is the light of my life and I will always protect her."

"Jillian, please don't worry. I want to be a good role model in her life too."

"If you're committed to getting to know her, then I'll support it—but for Melanie, not for you."

"I can understand why you're wary, but I promise you I'm done being a jerk. I've missed out on a lot and for that, I am truly sorry."

She eyed him with cautious regard. "Everyone can have a second chance, but don't mess it up. I won't give you a third."

CHAPTER 17

*M*elanie was finally asleep after three stories and one song. Jillian collapsed on the sofa, emotionally drained. Danny was flying home tomorrow, but he was calling Sunday night at six. Her cell pinged.

It was Brett. *How are you doing? Want to talk?*

She dialed the phone and he answered on the first ring. "Hey, how are you?" His voice soothed her.

"I'm fine. Danny wants to be in her life, so we've agreed to start with weekly phone calls. But it was interesting. She didn't refer to him as my dad and now that I think of it, she's never called him anything."

"Did he say something about that?"

"No, it just struck me as I was sitting here. But we'll see how things go. Who knows; he might lose interest unless his future wife really encourages him to keep up the calls. Oh, and he's thinking about coming here in the summer and spending a few days."

He asked, "Is that what you want?"

"As much as I was hurt, Danny was a decent man and it would be good for Melanie to know him and vice versa. If for no other reason than she can make up her own mind about him as she gets older. But I'm not letting down my guard and leaving her exposed to rejection or worse."

"She's lucky to have you as her mother."

Jillian didn't know how to respond to that. "What did you do tonight?"

"I stopped at my mom's and made her dinner for a change. She's not thrilled that I'm insisting we have Thanksgiving dinner out this year. I thought it would be easier than dinner for two, but it might make it harder for her since this is our first Thanksgiving without Dad."

"Dinner, in a restaurant?" Before she could censor her words, they tumbled out. "Come out to the farm for dinner with us. Our mothers would be great friends."

"Well, actually, they already know each other. I heard the news tonight that you hired her to work at Petals and to be clear, she had no idea we've been dating, but thanks for hiring her."

She laughed. "That's why her last name sounded so familiar. I never put two and two together. I guess I was distracted. I had just decided to put an ad in the paper and she walked in. I hope she likes it and doesn't get overwhelmed and quit before the end of the year. Besides February, May, and June, December is one of my busiest times."

His deep baritone laugh filled the line. "She loves a challenge and is looking forward to her first day more than you realize."

"I'm glad. Now what about the wreaths you and Melanie wanted to make to raise money? When did you want to get started? Tomorrow is nuts with floral arrangements but Friday would be good."

"That's perfect. I'll have plenty of time, I'm off, and I did tell Melanie we could start them Friday too. If you're comfortable, she's welcome to hang out with me while you handle your business."

She smiled. "How about we say you can work together and if needed, I can be called in to help with any details?"

"Deal. I'll call Mom when we hang up and see how she feels about dinner at your parents' if you're sure you want two guests."

"There's always room at the Morgan table for friends."

"Any chance we might progress from friends to something to a lot more serious?"

"Why, Brett, are you asking me to go steady?" She laughed.

"When you put it that way, it sounds so high school."

She continued to laugh and wiped a tear from her eye. It was the sweetest thing she had heard in a long time. "Let's discuss it on our next date."

"Friday night?"

"I'll check with Mom, but I'm sure that's fine."

"Great. Dinner at Antonelli's and a movie?"

She could hear the enthusiasm in his voice and loved that it matched her own. "Dinner sounds wonderful. I love Italian, but let's see what's playing or what else might be happening around town. After all, we live in Dickens and the Christmas season is gearing up; there might be something fun going on."

"True. I'll pick up the paper and we can see what's happening. Otherwise, dinner overlooking the lake will be romantic."

"I've been wanting to ask you if you'd be my date for Heather and John's wedding."

"I'd love to escort you. Is it black tie or just regular wedding attire?"

"A sport coat will be great." She tried to stifle a yawn.

"I heard that. You're tired, so we'll talk tomorrow, but I'm glad the conversation with Danny is behind you."

"Me too, and I'm looking forward to our date and spending time with you over the holiday weekend."

He paused. "Yeah, we're going to be spending a lot of time together. Hopefully you'll still like me by Sunday."

She chuckled. "I don't think you have anything to worry about. Night, Brett."

"Sleep well."

*B*rett would be picking Jillian up for their Friday night date soon and she still had no idea what to wear.

"Hey, Mom, should I wear a dress or slacks?" Jillian stuck her head out of her room and called down the hall in the direction of Melanie's room, where her mom was getting her daughter ready for bed.

"What are you doing besides dinner?" came the question in answer to her question.

"Maybe looking at the lights."

"Slacks and a sweater," she called back.

Satisfied her outfit was perfect, Jillian finished her makeup. Brett would be here any minute to pick her up for dinner and she didn't want to keep him waiting. She had straightened her curls and added a smoky blue-gray shadow to her eyes, which made them appear even bluer. With a final swish of lipstick and a spritz of perfume, she was ready.

There was a knock on the front door.

"I've got it, Mom."

*S*he swung the door open. Brett was standing on the top step, holding a single red rose. His eyes drank in the site of her: winter white slacks, a dove-blue turtleneck sweater, and sapphire drop earrings.

"You're so beautiful." He stepped into the living room and

handed her the flower and kissed her lips. "This is the first time I've seen you without curls."

"What do you think?" She wasn't fishing for another compliment; she really wanted to know what he thought.

His fingers slid through the long, silky strands. "Curls or straight, it looks wonderful."

Little feet pounded down the hall. "Brett." With a couple of long strides, Melanie jumped as if knowing Brett would catch her. Without hesitation, he scooped her up and gave her a hug. She wrapped her arm around his neck and looked at Jillian.

"Momma, you look so pretty."

"Thank you, baby." Jillian took her from Brett and gave her a kiss on her forehead. "You'll be good for Gram, right?"

She nodded. "Yes, and I've picked out my bedtime stories." She looked over her shoulder at Gram and giggled.

Jillian knelt on the floor. "Give me a kiss and I'll see you in the morning, okay?"

Melanie threw her arms around Jillian's neck and kissed her cheek. "You smell pretty too." She let go and looked at Brett, who bent down so she could repeat the gesture to him.

Mom took Melanie's hand. "Brett, are you going to the wedding next week with Jillian? We're having a sleepover at our place, so come to breakfast on Sunday for pancakes. Then the game and I think we're selling wreaths too."

He gave her a warm smile. He would love to be having a sleepover with Jillian, but they weren't there yet. "Thank you, Jean. I'd love to come for breakfast before hockey. Thank you."

"Good night, Mom, and if you need me, I've got my cell phone."

"Stop worrying and have a good time."

Brett held her coat so she could slip it on. "I'm ready."

He took her hand and said, "For whatever the night holds."

. . .

*S*trolling hand in hand, Jillian and Brett walked down Main Street in the direction of the Town Square and the gazebo.

"Dinner was delicious. I just love Antonelli's." She gave him a smile.

"It was excellent. I'm glad we went there, and the view was stunning."

Her heat skipped a beat. She hugged his arm to her. "But I think this is my favorite part of the night, being alone with you."

He stopped and pulled her to his chest for a kiss. "It wouldn't matter if we were in a crowd or like this; the favorite part of my day is to hold your hand and be with you too."

CHAPTER 18

*J*illian sipped coffee while she looked out over a quiet Main Street. Thanksgiving Day had arrived as a sunny but crisp morning, at least according to the thermometer outside her window. The house was quiet, with Melanie having spent the night at her grandparents'. The oven timer dinged. Time to check the pie. Her cell rang.

"Good morning, Jillian."

Brett was up early.

"Hi. Did you have fun last night with your friends?"

"Boston was nuts but we had a good time. I wish you had come to meet everyone."

She grabbed oven mitts and slid two pies from the oven. The crust was perfectly golden and the mouthwatering aroma of pumpkin and spice filled the air.

"Next time. I had the flowers for Heather and John's wedding on Saturday to finish and I wanted to get a jump on organizing the wreath supplies, since two elves are taking over part of my workshop again tomorrow."

"I'm looking forward to hanging out with Melanie and you."

She shut the oven off and left the mitts on the counter. "We are too. Speaking of spending time together, I hope your mom is looking forward to today. I can't imagine how hard it must be for her or you." She hesitated, waiting for him to respond.

"I'm doing okay. I'm not going to pretend it's easy, but I'm going over to Mom's in a while."

"Do you want to ride out to my parents' with me? I'm happy to drive you both home when you're ready."

"How about I pick you up instead? What time should we get out there, so I can let Mom know?"

"I was thinking twelve-ish. I like to take a walk in the fields with Melanie before dinner. She gets so excited, it helps to calm her down a bit."

"Would you care for some company on your walk?"

She was happy he couldn't see her do a jig in the kitchen. Melanie would be happy; heck, who was she kidding? She'd be thrilled.

"Jillian, is that a no?"

"We'd love to have you go with us."

"Great. How about I pick you up at eleven thirty?"

"I'll be ready. See you in a while." She put the phone in her pocket and hurriedly wiped down the counters. Then she dialed her parents' house phone.

"Hi, Momma! Guess what."

"Good morning to you too, munchkin."

"Morning, but guess what?"

"I have no idea. Tell me before you burst." She laughed to herself.

"I'm finally old enough to help Gram make the stuffing and put the turkey in the oven."

Jillian could picture her little girl talking a mile a minute while she stood on a stool at the kitchen counter to tear up the bread.

"And I used my hands to make the bread cubes." She took

a deep breath. "When are you coming? Are we going for our walk? Did you make pie?"

"Melanie, take a breath. Yes, to pie and our walk, and I'll be out around noon. Brett is picking me up and his mother is coming too."

"Wait a sec."

She could hear Mom speaking but wasn't sure what she was saying, and then she came on the line. "Hi, Jillian."

"Hey, Mom. Brett, Alice, and I will be out around noon. Do you need anything besides the pies?"

"No, we're all set. I'm glad you invited the Parsons to join us. When Alice was in the shop yesterday, she looked happier than I've seen her, not that we've been friendly for long, but giving a person purpose is a wonderful gift of hope for the future."

Jillian let that sink in for a moment. It was serendipity that Alice had walked past her shop moments after she put the help wanted sign in the window. "It will be good for all of us. I'll see you later, Mom."

*B*rett pulled up in front of Petals just as Jillian was coming through the front door, carrying a basket with handles. He hopped out of the car and hurried over to take it from her.

He brushed her lips with his. "Hi. Let me take that."

"Thanks." She locked the door and noticed his mother's car parked behind his. "Your mom wants to drive to the farm?"

She waved and grinned in his mom's direction. Alice returned the greeting.

"I think she wanted to give us privacy."

"That's sweet of her but not necessary. Holidays are about family, friends, craziness, and way too much food."

He put the container on the back seat and opened her

door. "I'm okay with having a few minutes alone with you. I was curious. Do you want to do something tomorrow night?"

"We could stroll downtown. A lot of shops will be decorated by then." She gave him a sidelong glance. "Could be romantic, strolling under the twinkle lights."

He kissed her cheek. "Then count me in." She waited while he got in the Jeep and closed the door. This was the first time a relationship was slowly evolving into a true romance, and he liked the pace at which it was unfolding. She was like the flowers she had in her shop. In the beginning, they were tightly closed but as time slipped by, they eased open, which only enhanced their beauty.

He took her hand once he began to drive. "I brought a couple of bottles of wine to go with dinner and some sparkling cider for Melanie. I hope that's okay."

Her eyes sparkled. "You bought kids' wine?"

"I can leave it in the car if you prefer. I just thought Melanie might like to have something special today too."

She leaned over and kissed his cheek. "That is thoughtful and she's going to be excited."

Pleased he had gone with his instinct, he smiled. "I think I'll have some with her if she'll share."

"She'll love that." Her smile dimmed as she looked out the window.

"Hey, what's wrong?" He squeezed her hand.

"You've been nicer to her than Danny has for her entire life and you've only known us a short time."

"You and Melanie are important to me."

She gave him a small smile. "It means more than you know."

In an effort to put a smile back on her face, he said, "How far are we walking today? I want to build up a big appetite before dinner."

"We walk out to a small pond where there's a bench. In the summer, ducks hang out and Melanie loves to feed them.

At this time of year, it's peaceful and we take a few minutes to say what we're thankful for, and we'll do the same on New Year's Day. We make a goal we want to accomplish for the upcoming year."

"Traditions are important. Is this something you did with your parents when you were a kid?" He checked his mirror to make sure his mom was still behind him as he turned down the road to the farm.

"We did, but now they go at a different time. It's a small family unit thing."

That was an interesting thought: Jillian, Melanie, and him, a family.

*B*rett took Jillian's gloved hand in his as Melanie ran ahead of them over the well-worn path through the meadow. The sun was high in the bright blue sky and the gentle wind swept away any sounds. It was as if they were the only three people left on earth. For a while, they just walked in companionable silence.

Swinging their clasped hands, she said, "This is nice." Sunglasses covered her eyes so it was hard to read her emotions, but he could hear the lightness in her voice.

"It is. I'm so glad I stopped buying supermarket flowers."

She gave a playful shudder. "Don't get me wrong; they have their place in the grand scheme of things, but purchasing an arrangement is more personal than a bunch in cellophane." He contained his smile; he wasn't going to confess there had been occasions his dad had bought super-market flowers and picked wildflowers. Dad didn't care. He was an equal opportunity flower shopper.

Melanie stopped and waited for them to catch up, then she took her mom's other hand. They continued down the path. Being with Jillian and Melanie made the grief he felt from losing Dad a little easier. And he could tell by the occasional pointed looks Jillian gave him, she knew when grief washed over him in waves.

"Hurry! There are geese on the pond; can you see them?"

They picked up the pace while trying to be quiet as they approached the water. In fact, the large open space in the middle that wasn't covered with a thin layer of ice was filled with geese.

"Is this part of their migration path?" he asked.

"We've never had a gaggle here before—or at least not this late in the season."

"Can I go closer, Momma?"

"Be careful."

Melanie pulled her hand free and crept close to the edge.

"Far enough." Jillian's voice carried and Melanie stopped.

Brett pulled his cell phone out and took a picture of Melanie with the geese and pond in the background. The sun created a halo against her golden curls.

"Go stand by her but don't look at me. I'd like to take a couple of candid pictures."

She walked toward the pond and over her shoulder, said, "Only if you promise to text them to me."

Her focus became centered on her daughter and together they both looked like angels, complete with halos. When Jillian knelt down next to Melanie, that was the money shot. A lump lodged in his throat. He wanted to have a picture of the three of them.

"Selfie time," he said.

The geese glided over the pond as if they were fine sharing this moment in time with the humans.

He picked Melanie up in one arm and Jillian stood close to him. He held his phone while she snapped the pictures. They were all smiles.

"Lemme see." Melanie squirmed, not to be let down but to get closer to the phone.

Was this what it could be like with a family, clowning for a camera and then wanting to see the evidence?

Jillian squinted and peered at the screen. "We look like a real family."

His heart constricted. It was as if she read his mind. It reminded him of pictures with him and his parents. Dad would really like his girls. He pecked Jillian's cheeks and hugged Melanie a little closer.

Jillian held out her hands to take Melanie. "They're great pictures, but we have to say our grateful statements before we can head home."

Melanie pulled them toward the bench. "Come on. We need to sit down."

She flashed him a smile.

He slipped an arm around her shoulders. "I like these traditions."

*

Jillian sat on the bench with Melanie between her and Brett. The innocent comment that they looked like a family stabbed her in the heart. It was something she had wanted for them, and Melanie was right. They did look like they belonged together. But now that Danny wanted to be a father to Melanie, what would that mean for her future with Brett? Would it come between them, as there were so many unknown variables?

Melanie wiggled on the bench. "Brett, you go first since this is your first time."

"Why don't you go first so I know what to say?"

"Okay. I'm grateful I have a swing set at Gram's house since we live in a 'partment and don't have room for one, and that we're gonna buy toys to help Santa."

She looked at Brett, her face shining and full of happiness. It eased the pain Jillian felt that they didn't have their own home with swings in the backyard, and she was proud of Melanie for adding helping Santa.

"Your turn, Brett."

"I'm grateful to have you and your mom as my new friends and that I'm coaching hockey." He leaned closer to Melanie. "And I'm grateful I've learned how to make wreaths with my favorite six-year-old."

She turned to Jillian. "Your turn, Momma."

"I'm grateful I get to be your mom and that our family is healthy." Her eyes held Brett's. She was also grateful for her new friend, but she didn't want to sound like she was just saying it. By the smile on his face, he had guessed what was left unspoken.

A flutter of wings drew their attention to the pond. The geese rose from the water and took flight in a southerly direction.

"Look. There they go." Melanie pointed as the last bird soared upward.

They sat and watched for a few more minutes before beginning the walk back to the farmhouse. She loved the leisurely pace of Thanksgiving, a day about the people in your life and how you chose to spend it.

Melanie was between them, holding their hands.

"Is there anything I can help with for the wedding on Saturday?"

Jillian said, "I have to decorate the ceremony site and set the flower arrangements up in the barn."

"Is that a big job?"

"I'm going to decorate an arbor set among the pines for the ceremony. It'll be draped with cream-colored sheers, greens from the trees, and holly berries. The arbor decorations will be able to withstand the cold without drooping. The reception's in an antique barn on the property. They finished renovations a while back and it's very romantic, with rustic elegance. The centerpieces look like old-fashioned lanterns and they'll have deep-red candles. On the tables, evergreens with red and white rose petals. As the final touch, sheers will be draped with more white twinkle lights."

"That's a huge undertaking." Brett gave her a concerned look. "Will you have time to get that all done?"

With a laugh, she said, "I just deliver the flowers and elements; the wedding planners will take care of the actual decorating. But I do need to decorate the arbor."

"Could you use an extra pair of hands?"

"You want to spend part of your Saturday morning before most people have had coffee helping me set it up?"

His smile grew and he nodded. "I think it sounds like fun, and then if Melanie and I need to make more wreaths, we can."

The house came into view. They'd be walking in the door within minutes.

"What do you say, Jillian? Could you use a helper?"

"If you really want to, sure. I'll never turn down an extra set of hands."

Melanie ran to the house.

"This has been the best Thanksgiving in a long time. Thanks for including me." He pulled her into his arms and kissed her tenderly.

She loved the spicy scent of his aftershave. She tipped her head back and looked into his hazel eyes. "The day just started." She ran her finger down his nose and bobbed the tip. "There's still food to eat, football to watch, and then leftovers to eat again before we roll home."

"As long as I get to do all of this with you and Melanie, I'm a happy man."

"You're easy to please." She stood on her toes and brushed her lips to his.

. . .

*S*itting on the plush overstuffed sofa with Jillian in the crook of his arm on one side and Melanie snuggled next to him on the other was nothing short of a surprise. If anyone had told him six months ago this is what his holiday would be like, finding happiness since losing his dad, he would never have believed them. The day was bittersweet but it was easier to bear spending the day with his mom, Jillian, Melanie, and her family.

"Mrs. Parsons, do you want me to read you a book?" Melanie slid off the sofa and crossed the room to stand next to her chair.

"If it's okay with your mom, you can call me Alice."

Melanie popped a little hand on her hip and looked at Jillian, who smiled at her little girl.

"Yes, you can."

Brett watched his mom scooch over to make room for Melanie. "What are you going to read?"

"My favorite book. It's about a mouse that lives in a teapot all by herself and her friends come for a tea party."

He could see that Mom was relishing the time with Melanie and it struck him that she was all he had anymore. He needed to make sure he didn't forget that as his future with Jillian and Melanie became a priority. But by looking at the smile on her face, he decided she was going to be an amazing grandmother someday.

Jillian jumped up and yelled at the television. Her team had just fumbled the ball. If she got this excited over football, he couldn't wait to see her at a hockey game.

"I was just thinking what if we got tickets for all of us to go to a Bruins game during Christmas break? Melanie would have fun and if everyone wants to go, we could make it a new tradition."

"I'd love to go to a game, but are you sure you want to go as a group?" She looked up from her spot next to him.

"Hey, does everyone want to go to Boston for a hockey game?"

Melanie's eyes grew wide and she squeaked out a yes, and Jillian's parents and his mom agreed it would be fun.

"That's settled. I'll call my contact at the organization this weekend."

The older set and Melanie went into the kitchen for cocoa.

Jillian cocked her head. "If it's late to get tickets, maybe the farm team in Providence would be easier to get, and for a weekend too."

He nodded. "Right, school."

Today had shown him what he had longed for without realizing it: Jillian, a family, a house of their own, and dogs—with more kids, of course. He had to wonder if it was normal to know so soon after dating someone, but there weren't any rules when it came to love.

"The game will be something fun for us to look forward to when winter starts to wear us down and cabin fever sets in."

He said, "Between Melanie's games and our adventures, we might wish for a snowstorm to keep us snuggled up at home, watching movies and eating popcorn."

"That's a great idea too."

He tapped his temple. "I've got my thinking cap on just to keep you and your little girl on adventures big and small."

"You do know we're kind of dull. You might get bored." A flash of concern clouded her blue eyes.

"The last word I would associate with either of you is dull. You're the most vibrant woman I've met in years."

With a soft laugh, she said, "Since we're alone, how about you kiss me?"

That was not an invitation he was going to let slip away. He lowered his mouth and nibbled hers. "With pleasure."

CHAPTER 19

*T*he next morning, Jillian listened as Melanie and Brett talked about each wreath theme. She had to smother her laughter as he discovered Melanie might be six but stubborn as a mule.

The shop door opened and Heather sailed in. "Hi, Jillian. I just wanted to check and make sure everything is on schedule and there aren't any glitches so far."

Jillian gave her a warm and reassuring smile. This was not the first nervous bride to come into the shop right before her special day.

"Can I get you a cup of tea? We can review the details if that would reassure you."

"I'd love tea but if you are sure we're all set for the wedding, we can skip going over it again. I think it would actually ramp up my nerves." She wiped the palms of her hands on her jeans.

"Have a seat and I'll be right back." Jillian slipped into the back room and set up the Keurig machine to brew the herbal tea. A blend of chamomile and peppermint was the trick. She added a drizzle of honey while she waited for it to finish brewing.

Brett and Melanie never looked up, intent on securing a plaid bow on a large wreath, but she knew they were both aware of her.

"Do either of you want a cup of cocoa or coffee?"

Melanie said without missing a beat, "Coffee with extra cream, hold the sugar, sugar."

"That sounds like something your grandfather says to Gram." The first mug sputtered to a finish.

Melanie giggled. "It is. Can I have cocoa, please?"

Brett smiled at her and winked. "Make that two, please?"

She smiled when she saw them together. Two peas in a pod. "You got it."

She pulled down two more mugs from the shelf and brewed up the cocoa before going back out front to Heather with the soothing tea.

"Sorry. I made cocoa for the elves in the back." She handed a mug to Heather.

"Is Melanie in the back with a play date?"

"No, she and her hockey coach are making wreaths to sell at the rink on Sunday. They've decided to raise money to purchase toys for the drive at the community center."

"What a nice idea, but did you say her coach is back there?" She raised an eyebrow. "Is there something you should be sharing with your best friend?"

"It's nothing." She sipped her tea and noticed Heather was still watching her.

"You're dating him, Jill. I need a distraction and your love life fits the bill, so spill it." She waved her mug in the direction of the back. "I know for a fact you never let anyone you're dating into your personal space, let alone let them spend time with your daughter. So there's more to this than *nothing*. And for the record, I'm not going anywhere until I get all the details."

Jillian glanced at the back room and lowered her voice. "Yes, we're dating, but it's casually romantic."

With a snort, Heather said, "There's no such thing."

"We only met about six weeks ago."

Heather's eyes grew wide. "You've been seeing this man for six weeks; he's spending time with Melanie, and still you say it's nothing? Doubtful. You like him and you know it."

"It's complicated. I'm a single mom and he's a single guy." She put her tea on the small table next to the counter. "We've had fun, but I still don't know how serious I should let it become. What if Melanie gets hurt?"

"I call BS. She is a small part of this, but if you like the coach and he's a good man, why can't you find what I have with John?"

"There's a difference. Hailey is older than Melanie and John loves her."

"True, but it's still taking a chance and isn't the bigger question *what if you get hurt*? You've said you haven't dated anyone for long since Danny, and he sliced your heart like freshly sharpened skates on new ice."

Jillian looked out the front window. It was still hard to admit how much it had hurt to have Danny turn his back on her and their baby. Now that Melanie was older, it would be worse if things didn't work out with Brett.

"That was six years ago."

Heather placed a hand on her arm. "But there are days it still feels fresh. I heard he was in town. Amy mentioned it when I picked up coffee on Wednesday."

"He wants to get to know his daughter after all this time, so he's going to start with regular calls and we'll see where it goes from there."

"That's good news, right? You've always wanted her to have him a part of her life. Every girl should have their dad around at least to have phone calls with."

"I know it's good for her, and seeing her with Brett has shown me how much she's been missing without a male figure in her life. You should see the two of them together.

They have fun and I don't need to run interference between them. He even watched her while I met with Danny, and I think Brett enjoyed it more than Melanie did. She got three bedtime stories out of him." She smiled when she thought about it.

"He sounds like a keeper. Do yourself a favor, Jill. Enjoy each day. After all the joy you've given people over the years with flowers and always lending a helping hand, you deserve to be happy." She finished the last of her tea. "And on that note and the tea, I think I'm ready to get back to the tree farm and check on the wedding planner. They're setting up the tables today." Heather stood up. She gave Jillian a broad smile and strode to the back room. "I think I'll introduce myself."

"Wait, don't say anything."

Heather just grinned. "Hi, Melanie."

Jillian stood in the doorway, waiting for the floor to open up and swallow her before embarrassment took hold.

Melanie glanced up from the workbench. "Hi, Heather. This is my coach, Brett, and he's my friend too."

She held out her hand. "It's nice to meet you, Brett. Will I see you at the wedding tomorrow?"

He shook her hand and smiled. "It's nice to meet you too and yes, I'll be there." His gaze lingered on Jillian.

Heather's eyes were glued on Brett and it was easy to see she didn't miss his loving look, as her eyes widened and her smile grew wide.

"I'm sure Jillian will be happy to introduce you to everyone. It's not a huge wedding, only about one hundred people, but I promise it'll be a good time."

"I'll look forward to it."

Heather beamed. She turned away from Brett and winked at Jillian as she mouthed, *He's cute.* "See you tomorrow."

Jillian followed her to the front of the store.

"Just because you're the bride doesn't mean I don't find you mildly annoying." She gave Heather a hug. "But I love you anyway. Now go get your nails done or something else bridelike."

"I like him. Don't let this guy get away; I've got a good feeling about him."

"You and your good feelings."

"Hey, look at what happened when I listened to my own inner voice. I'm about to marry an amazing man." She glanced at the wall clock. "I gotta run. See you tomorrow."

Jillian leaned against the counter as Heather left the shop. She had one thing right. Brett was super cute and nice.

While she was thinking of Brett, Alice walked in.

"Good morning, Jillian."

"Hi, Alice. The phones have been quiet so far and now that you're here, I'll start making a few arrangements."

"Sounds good." She put an apron over her head and tied it around her waist. "I'll let you know if I have any questions."

"Sure, just holler." She walked into the back. It was time to do a final check on the wedding flowers.

CHAPTER 20

The next morning, Jillian made the final walk-through of the barn for Heather and John's reception. There was nothing more that she could add; everything was perfect, right down to the gourmet chocolates at each place setting.

"Hi there." Brett crossed the room. "I put the last of the empty flower boxes in the van. Are you ready to take off so we can get dressed?"

"Before we do, I wanted to thank you again for dinner last night and the stroll in town. It was just what I needed to relax and unwind before the hectic holidays."

Brett gave her a heart-melting smile. "You're welcome, and thank you for asking me to be your date today. I'm looking forward to meeting your friends." He took her hand and gave her a twirl. "Do you dance?"

"I've been known to kick up my high heels occasionally. You?"

"I love to dance." He nuzzled her neck. "I can't wait to hold you in my arms and dance with you later today."

She gave a soft, husky laugh. "You might not say that if I step on your toes."

"It won't matter."

She gave him an apprising look. "Are you really this nice or should I be waiting to see the other side of you pop out?"

"Nope. One-dimensional kind of man. What you see is what you get."

The caterers entered the barn and with that, the intimate moment was gone.

"Keys, please?" She held out her hand. "I have to load the wreaths in the van for tomorrow and then get ready."

He kissed her cheek. "I'll help and then be back to pick you up."

*T*he rest of the morning flew by. Jillian was dressed in an elegant wide-leg pantsuit, but calling it a suit was too bland. It was a stunning deep-purple beaded jacket that showed a hint of cleavage and the lace of her camisole. Today, her curls were controlled soft waves around her face. The concession to the outdoor ceremony was black ankle boots with a low heel, easy to walk and dance in. She was ready and waiting for Brett when he walked up her stairs and through the open door.

Her heart stilled. He wore a deep-gray suit and crisp white shirt with a green tie. He was incredibly handsome.

He ran an appreciative eye from her toes to her curls. "You look gorgeous. Are you trying to outshine the bride?"

"Well, that would never happen; it's all about the happy couple. I just wanted to dress so I'd be warm outside and when we dance, I can slip off the jacket and be comfortable." She picked up her coat but he took it from her.

Before holding it open, he kissed her lips. "I won't be looking at anyone but you."

She smiled. "For courtesy, make sure you look at Heather when she's walking down the aisle and later in the reception hall."

"That, I can do." He held her coat while she slipped it on and fastened the buttons. He extended his hand and said, "Shall we?"

"Most definitely." Without a care in the world, they left her cozy apartment.

*B*rett liked sitting with his arm around Jillian during the ceremony and now at the reception. He had met so many people, he wasn't sure he'd keep all the names straight, but the smile on Jillian's face was all he needed. He had made sure to tell Heather she looked lovely and John that he was a lucky man. But it was Brett who felt he was the luckiest man alive with this beautiful woman by his side.

"Can I get you a glass of wine or something stronger?" He gestured to a short line at the bar.

"I'd love a poinsettia."

Confused, he said, "You want a flower?"

She shook her head and with a laugh, said, "No, it's the signature drink for today. Prosecco, cranberry juice, and orange liqueur." She placed a hand on his arm. "Trust me. It's delicious."

They strolled across the dance floor, fingers interlaced, in the direction of the bar. Brett saw Heather glance their way and gestured for her new husband to look. They both smiled. He didn't need anyone's seal of approval, but knowing Jillian's friends accepted them as a couple was a good sign.

After they had flutes of poinsettias, they strolled to the appetizer table. "How did you and Heather meet? I know you've known John forever since you both grew up in Dickens, but I think I heard someone say she's relatively new to the area."

"She opened The Library Cat Bookstore four, no, five years ago and she's a single mom too, so we bonded over shared struggles. She's really sweet and I'm thrilled she and John found each other." Her voice was wistful. "They make a great couple and now a family."

"They do look like a great couple." He kissed her cheek.

She slipped an arm around his waist and gave him a one-armed hug. "Are you having fun?"

"This is great."

"Then how about a spin on the dance floor since the new mister and missus have had their first dance?"

He smiled into her eyes. "I thought you'd never ask."

They crossed to their table and left their drinks and plates of appetizers. Brett took her into his arms for a slow dance. Swaying to the music with their bodies close, he could feel her heart beat, and her breath was sweet and warm against his cheek. The song moved from one into another and he was lost. She looked up.

"You're very light on your feet."

"So are you. It must have been all those years on the ice; we needed to be able to bop and sway on a razor-thin blade."

"I like this kind of sway almost as much."

He laughed as he held her closer. "Maybe more."

After a few more dances, they crossed the floor to enjoy the supper that was being served. At their table were a few other friends whom Jillian had known for years. Brett thought it felt good to be included like he was an old friend. Once the meal was over and they waited for cake, most of the people found their way to the dance floor or to chat with other guests.

He looked around the room. "Have you ever thought about getting married?"

She picked up her coffee cup and sipped. Was she stalling for time?

"I'm sorry. I shouldn't have been so blunt." He felt bad putting her in the hot seat.

"No, I like that you're direct and I've thought about it, but it's a lot to ask of a guy who might want to marry me."

"What do you mean? Because you're a business owner and work a ton of hours?"

"Melanie. If I were to get married, we're a package deal, and that's nonnegotiable. But it would be nice to have someone in my life, a real partner I could share my dreams with, work hard, and play even harder with."

"Would you want more kids?"

"Maybe one more. They're expensive. Especially if another one wants to play hockey or another equally expensive sport, or maybe even be musical." She laughed. "You have no idea how much money can evaporate from your wallet when you bring a baby home. But I wouldn't have changed a thing."

"Tell me one of your dreams." He warmed up her coffee from the carafe on the table.

"I'm saving to build a home on my parents' farm. They gave me a couple of acres; actually, it's not far from the pond we went to on Thanksgiving. I want the back of the house to overlook that field. Nothing huge, but a place where someday there'll be grandkids running around and watching the geese on the pond or dropping a fishing line."

"That sounds nice, and it's a perfect spot for a home."

Jillian pointed to Heather and John. "They've had some tough times but look at them, so in love and planning for their future. That is something I'd love to have someday."

He took her hand and brought it to his lips. "With love, everything is possible."

"You are such a romantic." She pulled him to his feet. "Dance with me?"

"My pleasure."

*B*rett pulled up in front of Jillian's store. The light she had left on in the front window welcomed her home. She was tempted to invite him up, but without Melanie in the other room, things could get steamy between the two of them and she wasn't ready for that—well, not yet. She unbuckled her seat belt.

"I had the best time tonight."

She leaned over and kissed him tenderly, which quickly turned into something with much more heat. She eased away, her heart racing and blood pounding in her ears. The attraction she felt was unmistakable and by the look of desire in his eyes, he felt it too.

With a catch in his voice, he said, "I'll walk you up."

She placed her hand on his as he pushed the car door open. "Brett, can we talk a minute?"

He closed the door and gave her a tight smile. "Of course."

She took a deep breath. "I really like you and as much as I want things to lead in a certain direction, I'm not ready. I know lots of couples after dating for almost two months would be physically closer, but I'm not ready for that yet. I felt I should be up front and not give you any mixed signals."

Relief washed over him. He cupped her cheek with his hand and caressed her chin with his thumb. "There are only two people in this relationship, and we get to decide when and how fast we move forward. If you're happy where we are for now, then that's fine with me. I love being with you and your daughter and I will never pressure you to do anything you're not ready to do. In fact, I'll wait for you to let me know you're ready to take the next step. I get to be with you, and that is really all that matters."

She exhaled and relief coursed over her. "You're a great guy and I know I've said it before, but this is the first real relationship I've had since Danny."

"Understood. Now, you're starting to shiver so we can hang out in the car with the heat on full blast, or I can walk you up and kiss you goodnight, or I'm happy to stay a little longer and maybe we have a hot beverage and then I'll leave. We've got another busy day tomorrow and your little one is going to keep us on our toes."

She laughed. "You know her so well. I'd love it if you'd stay and we could have something to drink—tea, cocoa, or something stronger. Your choice."

"I'd thought you'd never ask." He pushed open the door and came around to help her out of the car. A few snow flurries began to drift down. "I haven't kissed you yet in the snow."

She tilted her head to the side and lifted her face. "What are you waiting for?"

That was an invitation he wasn't about to pass up. He lowered his lips to hers, but before they met, he said, "For the record, I also want to kiss you in the rain and under the hot summer sun and falling leaves."

CHAPTER 21

$\mathcal{T}$he next morning, Jillian was packing a small tote bag with snacks and bottled water for after Melanie's game.

"Momma"—Melanie pulled a long-sleeved t-shirt over her head. It had her favorite mermaid princess on the front—"do you think we'll win our game today?"

"The league doesn't want you to focus on winning or losing. It's about developing the best hockey players you can be, and that means putting into practice what you've learned and being a good team player. If you do all of that, you'll be a winner."

It was easy to say that now, and there would be important games won and lost. Some would be a bitter pill to swallow, but it was part of life.

Jillian left the bedroom to make sure she had hand warmers in her jacket. She also needed thicker socks. She gave silent thanks to her mom for all the years hanging out in a freezer so she could pursue the love of the game. If her daughter loved the game as much as she had, many years of sitting in the stands were ahead for her. She longed to lace up and hit the ice, even if it were in a coaching position, but that would have to wait until Melanie was older. Right now, she needed her mom to be her cheering section.

"Munchkin, ten minutes before we have to leave."

"Okay, Momma. I gotta find my purple socks; I can't skate without them."

Oh jeez, did a six-year-old already latch on to her good luck charm? "Check your top dresser drawer."

"Found 'em."

With a smile and a laugh, Jillian thought, *Crisis averted.*

*W*hile Melanie warmed up on the ice, one of the fellow moms made a beeline to Jillian.

"Hi. Was it your daughter who made the wreaths and sold them outside the rink on Sunday?"

"Hi, Marie." She smiled and said, "It was. She was raising money for the toy drive."

A look of surprise flitted over Marie's face. "How did you get her to do it? I've been trying to find ways to get my kids involved in a project like that and all they want to do is play video games after school."

"It was Coach Parson's idea. He helped us make some wreaths, and he knew she loved it and came up with the idea to sell them to raise money. The tricky part was explaining to Melanie about the toy drive. I reminded her that with so many children Santa has to visit, he might need some help. She jumped at the chance once we said she could go shopping with us."

"If you're willing to provide direction, do you think the team could help out next year and do a toy drive on a larger scale?"

"I'm sure we can work something out, but we'll have to get permission from the booster club. Maybe we should talk about it at our next meeting. Since it doesn't directly benefit the team, it might not be something we can promote as a team event."

Marie grinned. "You leave that to me. I'll get everyone on board." She extended her hand. "Melanie has inspired me to do more."

As the woman returned to her normal spot in the stands, Jillian thought about her daughter and maybe instead of people wasting time on negativity, she could be a beacon for kindness. But what would the broken promises from Danny do to her? It had been a few weeks and he hadn't called. Not that Jillian had really expected him to, but it would have been nice for Melanie.

She zipped up her coat and watched Coach Richards slump to the bench and look down at the ground. That was odd. Brett was focused on the game. Concern propelled her to her feet and she made her way to the space behind the bench.

"Coach Richards, are you alright?"

He shook his head. "I'm just a little dizzy."

Jillian came around and took one look, then she gestured to the security guard standing near the front door. "Coach, I don't want to alarm the kids so I'm going to have the security guard walk you to the lobby and he'll call for an ambulance. Will that be okay?"

"I can't leave the game. Brett needs help."

"I'm here and I have a little experience."

He gave her a strained smile. "You do. Thanks."

Jillian quickly explained what was going on to the security guard, who put a supportive hand under the coach's elbow and helped him stand.

He handed her his whistle. "You might need this. At least you'll look official."

They left and Jillian turned her attention to the game.

Brett took advantage of a longer stretch of play to hustle down the length of the bench to her. He watched as the coach was ushered out of sight. "What's that all about?"

"He's not feeling well so good news! I'm your assistant for the night."

"Okay, you know what to do, right? Make sure the right kid gets on the ice when you tell them to." He smiled. "And feel free to dole out advice too. I know I can trust your feel for the game—"

She yelled, "That's it, Suzi. Take the shot!" She gave him a wink. "I hate to admit this, but I've been coaching from the stands." She was totally focused on the game now. She clapped her hands and called out more encouragement as the kids all clustered around the puck.

*B*rett kept one eye on the game and the other on Jillian. She was a damn good coach, so why had she been sitting on the sidelines this whole time? It would be better for the kids if she was out on the ice every practice. As kids came out of the game, she took time to speak with each player and offer them advice or encouragement. Not just Melanie, who listened to her mom's advice, but all the kids responded to her with the same rapt attention. They didn't do that with him. His admiration for her grew.

The rest of the game was a rapid-fire pack of kids racing up and down the ice, all chasing the same little black disc. How long would it take for them to realize they had a position to play? He thought back to the early years when he had started. It had come with maturity. Once one kid caught on, the rest would eventually follow.

The final whistle blew and Team Mites A, which was not his team, had won the game by a single goal, but when his kids asked, he and Jillian told them it was tied and they should be proud of how well they had played. They directed the kids to the line so they could high-five their opponents and tell them over and over, repeating a chorus of "*Good game!*"

Melanie skated over to Jillian and struggled with her helmet straps. "Did you see me, Momma? I tried to score but the puck bounced out. That goalie is good."

Brett hid a smile. It had been dumb luck the puck hadn't gone in the net and he had seen the surprised look on the goalie's face when it bounced back into play. Melanie was excited by the attempt, and wasn't that all any coach could hope for at this point in the development of the team?

His eyes met Jillian's. Her smile wasn't just on her lips but definitely shone in her eyes.

"You played awesome tonight. Are you ready to go home and have some dinner?"

"Yuppers."

"Go take what you can of your gear off and put everything in your bag and I'll come help with the rest after I talk to Brett."

Melanie skated to the edge of the rink and made her way to the locker room where her bag was stored. Jillian hadn't taken her eyes off her daughter until she was inside, and Marie pointed to Melanie and then to herself. She trusted Marie would keep an eye on her too.

"Are you going to check on Coach?" she asked.

"I will, and when I know something, I'll give you a call. By the way, thanks for jumping in there and taking care of things." He pointed to the ice. "You're good at this coaching thing and if for any reason Coach can't come back for our next practice, would you help out again?"

She touched his arm. "What, you don't want to wrangle a bunch of little kids by yourself?"

"Uh, no. I'm good but not quite that good. Plus, league rules require at least two adults." He winked at her. "And like I said, you're good company."

"Then I'll consider it."

"I'll call later and give you an update."

Jillian walked back a few steps. "We're going to the Christmas tree lighting in the town square on Saturday night. Interested?"

"Absolutely. What time can I pick you up?"

"We'll walk from our place since parking is at a premium. If you want to come over for potluck before that, we'll eat around six. Tree lighting is at seven."

"It's a date."

Jillian stopped right before the bleachers. "Talk to you later."

He tapped his index finger to his forehead in a salute. "Bye for now."

*B*rett was a little disappointed Jillian hadn't asked him to come over for dinner after the game. The more time he spent with her and Melanie, the more he wanted to spend with them. They were like cool, refreshing water and he was a thirsty man on a hot summer day. He pushed open the back door to his mom's and the smell of something wonderful instantly made his mouth water.

"Hey, Mom. What's cooking?" He entered the kitchen and was pleased to discover his mom was stirring a large pot of soup. "Any chance you want to take pity on your son and feed him dinner tonight?"

"No plans with the lovely Morgan ladies?"

"Not tonight. I think Jillian likes us to have a bit of space and you know, love is like a flower and to get it to grow and blossom, sometimes it just needs to do its own thing."

She set the wooden spoon aside. "Are you saying you're in love with Jillian?"

"And Melanie. They're a package deal, Mom." He picked up the spoon and gave the hearty vegetable soup a stir, letting his announcement sink in. But what kind of relationship could he have with Melanie if her father was in and out of her life? Would it sour his relationship with her?

"That's wonderful, and does she feel the same way about you?"

"I know she really likes me but we haven't said those very important words. Not yet anyway, and I'm not rushing into anything. But I'm thinking about a long-term plan." He gave his mom a look and then asked, "What do you think?"

"I've only known her for a couple of weeks, but she's very nice and that little girl of hers is too sweet for words. And not that you need to hear it from me, but I approve." She placed a hand on his arm. "Your dad would have loved her."

He swallowed the lump in his throat. "Thanks for saying that, and now that my love life has gotten the mom seal of approval, can we have dinner? I need to call and check on Coach in a while." He went on to explain what had happened.

"Did your team win?" She shooed him to the table and ladled up two bowls of the soup.

"We lost but the kids had a blast and Jillian stepped in and helped when Coach left. She's a natural with the kids and she hasn't lost her competitive edge."

Mom flashed him a confused look.

"Oh, you might not know, but she was training on the women's Olympic team seven years ago."

"Ah, and then came Melanie"—she placed the bowls on the table—"and she made the decision to change her life. Admirable. To be on the team meant she was one of the best in the country."

"She was the captain at Brown." He felt his pride surge.

"That had to have been a difficult decision," Mom said. "Your lives have strong similarities and I can see why you're drawn to each other. Not just the love of the game, but you both had to walk away from your dreams and start a new life. That takes a deep level of courage."

"If I had continued to play, I might have gone blind. It wasn't really a choice." He toyed with his spoon, pushing a chunk of carrot around his bowl.

"I disagree. You weighed your options and made the decision to have a long and healthy life. Some professional players risk it all because their ego won't allow them to change."

He let her comment sink in. Was it common sense or fear that had caused him to change the direction of his life? He chose to move to Dickens, be a physical therapist, and coach kids. Right now, it seemed like it was the smart choice. He had fallen in love with the most amazing woman and her daughter. He was right where he was supposed to be. Life did have a way of working out after all.

CHAPTER 22

*S*aturday night had arrived and Melanie had been bouncing all over the apartment because tonight they were going to the tree lighting.

A sharp rap on the door caused her to say, "I'll get it, Momma."

She flew down the stairs. Jillian could hear her say Brett's name and his response that she looked like she was ready for the town square. Their footsteps were quick on the wooden steps. She stood at the top of the stairs, watching Melanie hold his hand, urging him to go quicker.

"Come on. We're having homemade pizza and I helped make it, too."

"I can't wait." Jillian greeted him with a grin, pleased to see he was laughing and swinging Melanie's hand. "Can you tell we're a little excited? Santa is going to be at the tree lighting and we can't go until we have dinner. Hence the bouncing off the walls."

"I hadn't heard we were having a visitor from the North Pole tonight. That's pretty exciting." He laughed and gave her a light body check.

"I'm gonna ask Santa if he got the toys we bought. Do you think he knows I've been really good this year?"

"He knows everything, munchkin. Now, why don't you get washed for dinner so we can eat." Jillian looked at Brett and as soon as Melanie closed the bathroom door, she whispered, "Somehow I'm going to need to talk to Santa before she sees him to give him a heads-up about the toys she bought."

"Let me take care of that. You can distract her while I talk to him. Maybe he could even bring it up to her first—a thank you for helping him kind of thing."

"That's a great idea."

Melanie came out of the bathroom, waving her dripping hands.

Jillian shook her head and frowned. "Dry them on a towel please."

He bobbed his head in Melanie's direction. "You're on twenty-four seven."

She looped her arm through his. "You haven't seen the half of it."

*

*M*ain Street was twinkling in all its Christmas glory. Lights, white and colored, were in every shop window; trees lining the street were ablaze in white lights; potted trees sat beside each store entrance; the food trucks and souvenir vendors were operating around the town square, and it looked as if almost every person within Dickens was here.

"Is it like this every year?" Brett asked. He thought about the front of Petals. It had a wreath on the door, but it needed to be much more festive to live up to the other storefronts. But Jillian had been so busy, she just hadn't had time.

"Definitely. People love to see the Christmas tree lighting

and the chance to talk to friends and neighbors, and there's going to be a band playing too. There's something a little different each year." She steered him in the direction of the food trucks. "We need hot cocoa for three."

Melanie was talking nonstop and waving to classmates and some of her teammates too. "Where's Gram and Gramps?"

"They'll meet us by the gazebo."

Melanie's eyes filled with wonder as she stood open-mouthed, looking at the chair on which Santa would be sitting in less than thirty minutes.

"Do you think he'll bring his sleigh?"

"He probably left that in the North Pole so that his reindeer could rest up before Christmas Eve. Don't you remember last year, he arrived on the fire truck?"

She scrunched up her nose. "Oh yeah. I remember now he rode on the tippity top."

"That's right. He did."

*M*elanie took Brett's hand as the crowd of people grew larger and they got closer to the hot cocoa vendor. It was a gesture Jillian hadn't missed.

"I'm going to check with my parents to see if they want cocoa."

She sent a quick text as they moved up in line. She got a return with the number three. She held it up to Brett. "I think your mom is with them."

"A good possibility. She was planning on coming."

Jillian placed the order for six cups and Brett handed her cash to pay for them.

"Thank you."

A moment later, she was holding two cardboard trays. She

tilted her head toward the gazebo. "Off to find your grandparents."

"And to see Santa." Melanie's eyes were as bright as twinkle lights.

"Melanie," Brett asked, "do you know what you want to ask Santa for Christmas?"

She nodded and beamed. "And I've been super good, so I know he'll bring me just what I want."

Jillian winked at Brett. "She has asked for a new two-wheeled bicycle that is purple and has a basket."

"No, Momma. I changed my mind. I have something else I want even more."

"What is it?" This was news. Melanie had finished her list weeks ago.

She shook her head. "I can't tell you, only Santa. He'll know just how to get it for me."

Now Jillian felt a stab of worry. What if it was one of those high-demand toys, the ones that were always impossible to get after Thanksgiving? Unless it was something she could get Danny to buy for her. But maybe she wouldn't mention it to him. No matter what, tonight was special and before long, the magic of Santa would melt away.

"Are you sure you don't want to give me a hint?"

Again, Melanie shook her head. "I can't tell anyone except Santa. It's gonna be the best present ever."

Jillian knew that look on her face. At least for now, she wouldn't tell her mother anything.

"Okay, keep your secret, but when you tell Santa, make sure to speak clearly so he can understand you."

"I will."

Jillian's only hope was to be close enough to hear what she said and then if luck was on her side, she'd still be able to find it. Melanie asked for so little, Jillian wanted her to have that one specific item under the tree on Christmas morning.

Brett arched a brow. She gave him a short nod and tapped her ear. She'd find a way to hear what Melanie asked for.

*O*nce they reached the gazebo, it only took a few minutes to find her parents. She was glad to see Alice was with them. Mom gave Jillian a cursory look, as if seeing the tension on her face. She'd have to work on masking her facial expression.

Brett touched her arm as Melanie told everyone within hearing range that she was going to see Santa. "I'm guessing you have no idea what Melanie's going to say?"

"No. All she's talked about for two months is the bike. This is out of left field. She only ever asks for one gift. I used to make a list a mile long when I was a kid, so I hate to disappoint her. I've got the bike at my parents' house and now I'll have to try and track down this mystery gift."

He took her hand and gave it a reassuring squeeze. "I'll help. She won't be disappointed on Christmas morning."

"I appreciate your support." She leaned in with a chaste kiss. "Are you still going to try and get to Santa before Melanie about the toy drive presents?"

"Are you kidding? There is no way I'm going to let her be disappointed either. If I can't catch him before he sits down, I'll find a way to let him know. Don't worry."

She tapped her hot cocoa to his and in a hushed voice, said, "Here's to us saving Christmas."

"Momma, is it almost time for Santa?"

Jillian looked at the clock on the church steeple across the street. "In just a couple of minutes, we should hear the fire trucks."

Melanie danced around the adults and said, "Alice, have you sent in your Santa letter yet?"

Alice's grin grew wide. "Not yet, but I still have time, don't I?"

"I guess so. But don't wait. He has to have time to make it."

"Thanks for the reminder. What are you going to ask Santa for tonight?"

Melanie gestured to Alice to come closer. She said, "Oh, I see. And does your mom know?"

"Nope. Nobody but me and Santa. Otherwise it wouldn't be a secret."

Jillian cringed. Her mom's eyes widened.

The first wail of a fire truck could be heard coming around the corner. It was headed in their direction.

"Santa!" Melanie yelled.

The man in the red suit and long white beard was riding on top of the ladder, holding on with one hand and waving enthusiastically with the other, calling out *ho ho ho* as the crowd clapped.

Melanie was awestruck and a pang of sadness hit Jillian in the heart. In a few years, this would be old hat and her little girl would no longer believe in the magic of Christmas or all the other mythical characters that enriched childhood with wonder.

"Momma, Santa waved to me."

"I saw that." She picked Melanie up so she could see better, and Melanie kept waving. Her smile was so big, it couldn't stretch any farther.

"Let's get in line so we can be near the front."

Melanie leaned toward the gazebo while in her mom's arms. Jillian set her down and said, "Hold tight to my hand."

They found a spot near the front of the line. Brett was making his way around the side of the bandstand to have a quiet word with the man of the hour.

They were third in line. Jillian caught Brett in the crowd and he gave her a thumbs-up. That was one worry off her mind. Melanie tugged her hand.

"Momma, I can go up by myself this year."

"I know you can, but I want to be able to take a couple of pictures. Is that okay?"

She nodded as they took a step closer. The little boy in front of them waited patiently until it was his turn, and then Melanie took another step forward.

She was jumping up and down. "It's my turn next."

Jillian took out her phone. "I'm ready for your photo shoot."

"Momma, should I have brought Santa a cookie? He might be hungry."

She smothered a smile. "I'm sure he's had dinner."

Melanie looked behind her. "It's a long line."

"Everyone wants to ask for their wish."

Swinging their joined hands, she said, "I want to make sure he got the toys and ask for my gift."

The little boy beamed as he slid off Santa's lap and hurried over to his mom.

Melanie released Jillian's hand. She stood in front of Santa Claus.

"Hello, young lady, and what's your name?" He helped her onto his lap.

"I'm Melanie Morgan."

"Oh, you're Melanie. I'm so glad you came to see me. I wanted to thank you for the toys you donated to help me. That was very generous of you."

Her blue eyes became wide like saucers. "You're welcome, Santa."

Jillian took a step closer to take a picture and hoped Melanie was about to tell him what she wanted for her special gift.

He gave a hearty *ho ho ho*. "And what can I bring you this year?"

"Well, I was gonna ask for a purple bike but I've changed my mind." She looked at Jillian and leaned in closer to him.

Jillian strained to hear the next words.

"I'd like for you to bring me a daddy, the kind who really likes me and vanilla ice cream and rainbow sprinkles, not rocky road." She wrinkled her nose. "Yuck."

Santa looked at Jillian briefly before speaking. "I'm glad you mentioned the bike. I thought I saw that next to your name on my nice list."

"I'd like a daddy for me, and Momma could use a best friend forever too."

"That's a tall order, but I'll see what I can do."

"If you can't, it's okay. Momma says it's important to make a heart wish." She gave him a hug. "Merry Christmas, Santa." She slipped down and waved as she walked away.

She didn't realize Melanie adored Brett and had chosen him for her dad. Jillian wiped her damp cheeks with her glove and gave Melanie a bright smile. She swallowed the lump in her throat. "Let's go find Gram and Gramps."

CHAPTER 23

Stunned was the only way Jillian could feel as the family strolled downtown, enjoying the lights and waiting for the final magic moment of the tree lighting. It wouldn't be long now until she could go home and figure out how to prepare Melanie for the disappointment she was bound to feel on Christmas morning.

Brett squeezed her hand. "Are you okay? What was Melanie's wish?"

She shook her head. "Can we talk about it later?"

A look of confusion raced over his face but he quickly replaced it with a smile. "Sure. No problem."

She felt terrible holding back what she had heard, but there was no way she was going to tell him that Melanie wanted a daddy for Christmas and she chose him. Honesty was the foundation for any relationship, but until she could talk to her mom, she needed to keep it to herself.

"Time for the tree lighting. Let's go get a good place so we can see." Jillian forced her tone of voice to be upbeat even though it broke her heart that Danny had broken his promise to her again. He had stepped up with a solitary dish of ice cream, but that wasn't being a dad and Melanie knew it, too.

Melanie stood between her grandmother and Alice as the countdown began. Dad had his arm around Mom and Brett slipped his arm around Jillian's waist and held her close. This was what a family should look like, she thought. But what if she and Brett imploded? They were so new to dating, there was no way to tell at this point if it was going to stick. She glanced at Alice. She was just beginning to rebuild her life, make friends with her parents, and she was a terrific employee. The ripple effect of a breakup between her and Brett would hurt a lot of people. It wasn't just about the two of them.

The crowd called out, "Three, two, one!" The lights went from the bottom to the crowning star on top in a riot of colors, and people began to clap and whistle.

"Momma, it's officially Christmas and now we need to get our tree tomorrow. Can we, please?"

"We'll have to see. I have some things to get done before we do that."

Melanie's face fell.

"Don't worry, munchkin. We'll get our tree very soon."

"If you want, we can go and get our trees at the same time." Brett held her a little closer.

A half hour ago, Jillian would have jumped at the chance, but right now, she needed some space from whatever had developed between her and Brett.

It was like everyone just assumed they'd be one happy family, but no one was asking Jillian what she wanted, and didn't she need to figure that out before this went any further?

As much as she hated to do it, she said, "Can I call you tomorrow and let you know? I really need to do a few things that I just can't put off."

His hazel eyes were filled with questions. "Yeah. I'll be around most of the day and can be flexible."

Her heart ached. "Thanks for understanding."

For her ears alone, he said, "I don't know what happened. Did I do something to upset you?" He tucked a curl under her knit cap.

She shook her head. "No, it's nothing like that. I promise." She looked away. She couldn't stand to see the doubt that lingered in his face.

"Melanie, are your feet cold?"

"Not anymore."

With a short laugh, Jillian said, "You can't feel your toes anymore?" She swept her up into her arms. "You're getting so big, but I think it's time for us to go home and call it a day. A warm bath, and how about we have three stories tonight."

Melanie shook her head and held up four fingers with an impish grin. "How 'bout four?"

Jillian set her down and said, "We'll see after we get home. Say good night."

Melanie gave hugs to everyone but with Brett, she slipped her hand into his for the walk home. If that wasn't a clear signal as to what she wanted, nothing would be.

*B*rett walked along the sidewalk with Jillian and Melanie. It was the same walk they'd made earlier in the night, but now he felt as if a glacier had come between him and Jillian and he had no idea why. He tried to think back. Had he said or done something stupid? He came up empty. They were having a great time. Even Santa remembered to mention the toy donation.

Brett would do anything for these girls.

"Are you going to the rink tomorrow?"

She didn't look at him. "No, I don't think there'll be time."

"Momma, I wanna skate." Melanie yawned as her steps slowed.

Brett picked her up. "You're tired."

She nodded and placed her head on his shoulder. It made his heart melt a little more. If he hadn't already fallen in love with this pint-size person, he would have in that moment.

"Do you want me to take her?" Jillian held out her hands.

"No, she's fine." He gave her a smile. "Makes me feel a little like a hero."

"She's gotten heavy."

"I've got her." He longed to ask again what had happened earlier, but he needed to be patient. There would be time for that later.

Jillian withdrew her key and unlocked the door. They climbed the stairs without conversation and the tension grew. Once inside, she slipped Melanie's coat and boots off while Brett held her, but at this point, the girl was sound asleep.

"I'll lay her on the bed if you want to pull back the covers."

Jillian flicked on the hall light to illuminate the tiny bedroom decorated in purples and princesses, right down to the purple lace netting that served as a tent over the head of her bed. It was a true haven for a little girl. He placed her gently on the covers and she turned on her side without ever opening her eyes.

He pulled the covers up and whispered, "Sweet dreams, Melanie."

Jillian adjusted the covers, switched on the nightlight, and finally followed Brett down the hall to the living room.

"Can you stay for a while?" Her voice was soft but her eyes avoided his.

"Yes. I think we should talk about what happened tonight."

She moved into the kitchen and asked, "Something to drink?"

"No, thank you."

"Let's sit down." She walked to the sofa and perched on

one end. She turned so her back was against the arm, a clear indication she needed space between them.

He sat in the middle, close enough so he could touch her hand, although he didn't. He waited for her to say what was on her mind.

She looked at him, her voice steady. "Brett, I'm afraid I let things between us go too far. I don't want any of us to get hurt if we continue to see each other on a personal level."

He felt as if the air had been sucked from his lungs. What was she talking about?

"Jillian, what happened to make the turnabout?"

She looked away and then back at his chin. "We aren't looking for the same things. I see how you look at me, and I want to keep things casual. If we keep seeing each other, Melanie's going to get more attached to you. In the long run, it's easier to go back to being coach, player, and parent." He knew she was lying and it tripped on her tongue and shattered his heart to hear those words.

"What are you talking about? I care for you and Melanie and if you think I'd hurt you or her, you're wrong. I'd do anything to protect both of you. She's an amazing kid and I love her little old soul and her kind heart."

"See, you confirmed my point. You've gotten too attached to her and if we get more serious and then you leave, it will crush her."

"Do you think we want different things out of life? That I'd block her relationship with Danny? Because that couldn't be further from the truth. She has a right to have a relationship with him."

"You don't understand."

"What did Melanie say to Santa? Because that is what this is all about. What was her wish?"

Jillian got up and walked to the window. "She wants a real dad, one who doesn't like rocky road ice cream."

"What does ice cream have to do with anything?"

"She thinks rocky road is yuck. Her words, not mine."

What did ice cream have to do with them breaking up? "Well, she's not wrong there, but I still don't get it."

"When she saw Danny, that's what he ordered, and she had vanilla with rainbow sprinkles."

"Just like what I order." Now the fog was lifting. "I know that Danny has been out of her life, but I want us to explore the possibility of long term, the three of us."

She shook her head. "I can't. I've already had one person walk out of our lives. I can't risk it now."

He crossed the room and took her hand. Gently, he tipped her face up to look at him. How could he explain to her that he wasn't a walking out kind of guy? He was right where he wanted to be and while he wasn't ready to make a declaration —it was too soon for that—what they had together, and the relationship between the three of them, was a future he didn't want to step away from.

"I get it. You've been hurt and it's scary to let go."

She wrenched her hands away. "So you understand why we need to just be friends?" She blinked away the tears on her lashes.

He slowly shook his head. "I don't. I don't walk out on the people I love."

"That could change."

"Let's be honest for a minute. You care for me. I see it and feel it." He tapped the center of his chest. "When that sweet little girl put her words out there, it scared the heck out of you too. It made you aware that we all have a lot to lose, but isn't love worth the risk?"

"I don't know. I'm confused."

"Have I ever given you a reason to think I'll hurt either of you? I'm not Danny. I show up. I call." Those words pierced his heart. He wanted her to say that she was willing to go all in with him to face the future, whatever might come. Just like when they had coached the game, they were a strong team and he knew how to be a team player. All he needed was the opportunity to prove it to her.

"It's okay to be confused as our relationship evolves. I will always be here for you, whenever you're ready to talk. Right now, I'm going to give you space to think. Call me when you're ready. I'll be waiting."

She nodded but didn't speak.

He grabbed his coat and stopped at the top of the stairs. "Jilly, I'm not anything like him."

*

Calling her Jilly had almost been her undoing. After the door clicked behind him, she sank to the sofa and pulled the soft afghan over her. She was still overwhelmed by having heard those words—Melanie picked Brett to be her daddy. But it didn't seem to matter what Jillian needed or wanted. How could she expect Brett to understand she had given him a free pass to walk away from them? But she had feelings of loss already. She wasn't sure if she wanted to be with him because everyone else wanted her to or if she really did care for Brett.

Her cell rang and she didn't want to get up and answer it. There would be time tomorrow to talk to whoever. The message alert chimed. A few minutes later, a text message pinged. Obviously, someone was being persistent.

She crossed the room. Both the voicemail and text were from Mom.

I know you're upset. Call me tonight.

Might as well get it over with.

CHAPTER 24

"*H*ey, Mom." Jillian settled back on the sofa with her legs curled underneath her.

"I'm not going to ask what's wrong. Just tell me what is going on. But first, are you alone?"

"Yeah, Brett left a few minutes ago." She plucked at a strand of yarn on the blanket. "I broke it off with him tonight."

"Do you want me to come over?"

She could picture her mom already pulling on her coat, ready to come to the rescue with a cup of tea and a hug.

"No need for you to come over tonight. We can talk now." Her voice wavered when she thought she had just curtailed her chance for a happy life.

"Did you have a fight?"

"Nothing like that. Remember how Melanie said she had to see Santa because she had changed her mind about what she wanted him to bring her for Christmas but she didn't want to tell us?"

"Yes, go on."

"Well, Brett went in search of Santa before Melanie was going to sit on his lap to give him a heads-up about the donated toys. He thought if Santa brought it up first, it would make a huge impact on her."

"That was a thoughtful thing to do. So did he mess it up and not get to him in time?"

"No, that was the first thing Santa said to Melanie when she sat down. Her smile was as bright as the sunshine midday in July. It was after that she shocked the heck out of me." She stopped pulling the yarn and continued. "She asked for a dad, and she wasn't referring to Danny. That was clear."

"Oh, I take it she was insinuating Brett?"

"You guessed it. When I heard her ask Santa, there was such longing in her voice. I realized I let him get too closely entwined in our lives and it opened us up for him walking out when he got tired of being the family man."

"Has he ever said anything like that?"

She could hear the sharp tone in her mom's voice. "Not exactly, but I have no idea how long he plans on staying in Dickens. Yes, his mom is here, but she could decide to move back to Boston, and then what's keeping him here? Nothing. He could get a job as a PT for professional sports teams. I wouldn't want to hold him back."

"Did he say he was unhappy with his job?"

"Well, he hasn't, but like me, he walked away from hockey and his dream of going pro after he got hurt. If he wanted to find a job with a team, well, I'm not going anywhere. I won't uproot Melanie for that kind of a lifestyle."

"Seems to me like you've made a lot of decisions for him without asking what he wants."

"And what about what I want? I feel like everyone around us has decided Brett and I make a great couple, but no one's stopped to ask me if Brett is who I want as my love. Besides, Melanie needs stability, roots, and that's here in Dickens with her grandparents and mom."

"She does need stability, but that comes from you being

happy. Don't you see that? Jilly, I've seen you with Brett and you've been happy since you started dating him."

"Danny left me because he didn't want to be a father and I can't expect Brett to step in and fill his shoes." Tears welled up in her eyes and she blinked them away.

"What if you didn't have to ask but it's what he wants? Are you saying you don't have strong feelings for him?"

"That's not the point."

"It is the point. I want you to think about something. Put yourself in my shoes and Melanie in your place, twenty-five years into the future. What would be your advice to her? Tell her to close herself off from the possibility of a wonderful future with a great guy and protect her heart at all costs, or would you encourage her to take the chance, that with great risk comes great reward?"

"You nailed it, Mom. The possibility of…" She sat up straighter. Mom did understand.

"Jillian, so you're looking for a guarantee in life?" She gave a snort. "I hate to let you know, but there isn't one. The only thing we know for sure is we get one life to live and I suggest you think about how you want to live yours and what you want to teach Melanie. You need to think about what *you* want and need."

"I did the right thing." She threw the blanket off and crossed the window to look out over a quiet Main Street.

"Did you stop to think that maybe the reason we all think you're a perfect couple is because you complement each other? Long-lasting relationships are all about balance. I would encourage you to sleep on it before you plant your feet in water and it turns to ice."

"The ice has already formed." She closed the blinds and flicked on a lamp.

"True love can thaw even the hardest of icy hearts. Think about it and then make your decision. But I would strongly encourage you to not freeze him out of your life entirely."

"He's still Melanie's coach and we'll find a way to be friends. Besides, it's too late. He knows we're through."

"Come for breakfast tomorrow and we can talk some more."

"Thanks, but we're going to stick around the house and get ready to put our tree up and if I decide we're going to Gridley's to pick one out, do you and Dad want to tag along?"

"Come for pancakes, please?"

She heard the resignation in her mom's voice and it weighed on her like she had also let Mom down. "I'm sorry." It did sound nice to be home for breakfast. "Alright, we'll come."

"It's not too late. Call him."

"Good night, Mom."

"Sleep well, Jillian."

The call ended and exhaustion washed over her. This weight was heavy on her shoulders and maybe a good night's sleep would give her a better outlook. She knew it was the right thing to break things off with Brett, but how was she going to handle Melanie when she asked for him?

*

The next morning, Brett wandered around his apartment, still dumbfounded that Jillian wanted to end things. He didn't have any choice but to wait and hope she changed her mind. Instead of hanging around, he'd spend some time with his mom and decorate.

On the way to her place, he had to drive past Petals. His eyes were drawn to the second floor and to where Jillian parked her Subaru. No lights and no car.

He had an idea, and he was sure they had at least an hour, if not two, if she had gone to her parents' for breakfast. That was if he could enlist his mom's help to pull off a little surprise.

"*B*rett, grab that extra box of lights on the porch, and I think that will give us enough decorations for the exterior of Petals. Where are we going to get a tree on short notice?"

"I called Gridley's and they have cut trees we can buy and I paid over the phone. Someone's going to be bringing it by the store."

"I still can't get over how the small town of Dickens has remained a true community when so many places have lost that friendly feeling over the years. When your dad and I were looking to leave Boston, this was the only place we considered. I'll never forget it; we were having lunch in Dorrit's Diner and once we met Amy, all those years ago, we knew this was a wonderful community."

He closed the back door and slammed the hatch shut. Leaning against the Jeep, he said, "I want to make those kinds of memories with Jillian. Like what you and Dad shared."

"I've seen the way Jillian looks at you. It's the way your dad looked at me." She gave him a quick hug. "Have some faith."

"If Dad were here, what advice do you think he'd give me?"

"One word. Patience."

He rubbed a hand across his face and pushed off from his SUV. "Ready?"

She rubbed her hands together and chuckled. "Ever since you called this morning, I've been ready. Jillian is such a sweet girl and I see how much she gives back to the community, little ways she doesn't think anyone will notice, but that girl has a big heart."

After a short drive, they arrived at Petals. Brett and Mom

unloaded the Jeep, putting all the bags and boxes on the side-walk close to the building. He divided everything into what was needed where. First, lights around the windows and door.

"Shoot, we don't have an extension cord. Mom, can you walk down to Dickens Hardware and pick up two?"

"I'll be back soon. Anything else you think we might need?"

"No."

As she strode down the street, a pickup truck with the Gridley's Tree Farm logo pulled up. To Brett's surprise, John hopped out of the driver's seat and Heather got out of the passenger seat.

"Wanna give me a hand, Brett? I put the trees in tubs and they're kind of heavy."

He crossed to the back of the truck, where there were two tubs on their sides and a bunch of greens in the bed. "John, I paid for a tree, not all this."

He slapped Brett on the back. "Are you kidding? Heather and I wanted to add a little extra, and I'm pretty sure you can use some extra hands to make the magic happen, too."

Brett's throat tightened. "Thanks, and you're right. I want to be long gone before Jillian gets home."

He pulled out the first tub and placed it next to the front door. John did the same with the other tub. Heather brought out greens and then pulled a small ladder out of the back of the truck.

"You came prepared."

"My wife"—he looked at her and smiled—"is a whirl-wind, and when she heard me talking about your order, she was coming with me to help."

Brett grabbed a string of lights and wound them around one tree and up the door casing, where he added a new set to go down the other side and around the other tree. While he was stringing lights around the front windows, Heather stuffed boughs of greens into the window boxes and added deep-red bows to their fronts. Meanwhile, John was adding greens around the door. They were decorating in record time. Mom returned with a large tote bag.

Her brow arched as she looked from Heather to John. "I wasn't sure of the length, so I picked up a few. Whatever we don't need, I can take back."

"Mom, these are friends of Jillian's, Heather and John Gridley. We went to their wedding right after Thanksgiving."

"And we're your son's friends too." John shook her hand. "It's a pleasure to meet you, Mrs. Parsons."

Heather shook her hand too. "We wanted to help Brett decorate."

She surveyed the front of the store. "You got a lot done while I was gone. What's next?"

"We need bows on the treetops and ornaments." Brett pointed to a box. "I started getting them out but wanted to finish the greens first."

"Don't worry, son; I'll work on the trees. You can get the lights hooked up. Oh, and I called Jean. Jillian and Melanie are at the farm and she'll make sure they don't leave until I tell her it's all clear."

Brett dropped a kiss on her cheek. "Good thinking, and thanks."

The foursome worked in silence, getting everything to look just right and complement the window display that Jill had created on the inside. Brett stood back to admire their handiwork.

"Guys, come take a look."

Heather and John, along with Mom, joined him on the sidewalk. It looked like a scene out of a magazine, right down to the lifelike cardinal perched on the window box. He took his mom's hand and squeezed.

With a catch in her throat, she said, "To symbolize your dad is here too."

He blinked away the tears that formed. With a lump in his throat, he said, "It looks amazing. I can't thank you enough for all your help today. This is above and beyond what I had expected."

"Welcome to small-town life, Brett. Dickens is a special place. We take care of our own, even when someone is new to town. When they fit, we know it." He patted his shoulder. "We're going to take off and I'm guessing we're keeping this on the down-low as to who played elves today?"

"That's the plan unless someone saw us and gives it away."

"We worked fast, so hopefully no one will squeal," Heather said. "She's lucky to have you."

"Thanks." Now if only she'd realize that and let him back into her life.

The Gridleys drove away and he picked up the last of the boxes and put them in his Jeep. "Mom, go ahead and call Jean, then let's grab an early lunch at the diner."

"And then maybe you'll tell me what's going on between you two. That look on your face tells me something's happened and I can't help if I don't know."

"There's nothing to tell; a minor bump in the road and for now, I'd like to keep it to myself."

She patted his cheek. "I'm here if you need me."

"I know, and I appreciate that. I'm not worried; it will all work out." He wished he felt the same confidence that was in his voice.

CHAPTER 25

*J*ill drove down Main Street toward Petals. She slowed the car. "What the heck?"

"What's wrong, Momma?" From her booster behind Jillian's seat, Melanie strained to look out the windshield.

"Nothing's wrong, munchkin, but it seems Santa's elves were busy while we were gone. The front of our store is all decorated."

"I wanna see." She squirmed.

"Patience. As soon as I park the car, we'll be able to check it all out." She pulled in next to the building and before the car was off, Melanie had popped her seat belt and was climbing between the front seats.

With a laugh, Jillian said, "I guess you're excited. Come on, but stay on the sidewalk."

Melanie slid out the driver's door and raced around the side of the building. When Jillian caught up to her, she had her hands clasped together and gushed, "Look, Momma! Isn't it pretty?"

The entire front of her store was decorated, right down to a little cardinal in the window box, and then she saw the trio of white doves. Her heart constricted but a smile graced her lips. Brett.

"How did it all get decorated? Was it Santa's elves?"

She placed her hand on Melanie's shoulder, her heart thudding in her chest. She broke things off—but could the doves represent the three of them? Could he love her as much as she knew she loved him?

"I would guess it was his helpers. The elves are in the North Pole, making toys."

"Can you take a picture of us so we can send it to Gram and Gramps?"

She withdrew her cell from her coat pocket and turned Melanie so her back was to the storefront. This was something she wanted to have too. The gesture was thoughtful and heartfelt.

"Smile."

Melanie mugged for the camera and when they were done, they checked to make sure they got a good one.

"We should call Brett to see if he wants to come over."

"Honey, he's busy today, but I'm sure he'll see it soon." She pulled open the door to the stairs. "You know what this means, don't you?"

"Nope."

"We'll need to get our tree and put it up before it gets dark so the windows upstairs look as festive as they do downstairs."

Melanie clapped her hands. "We're gonna chop it down today?"

"After lunch, and your grandparents will meet us there too."

Melanie clomped up the steps. "Can I call them?"

"Absolutely."

Before handing over the phone, Jillian sent one of the pictures of them outside the store to Brett. Her fingers paused over the keyboard. Should she include a message? She hit send. No text, just the picture.

A one-word reply came back. *Beautiful!*

❦

The next afternoon, Melanie raced ahead of Jillian to the rink. Hockey practice was going to start in a half hour and the little whirlwind couldn't wait to get on the ice. She struggled to open the heavy door and urged Jillian to catch up.

"Come on, Momma! I want to skate. Tonight, I hope I get to practice hitting the puck at the goalie. I wanna score a lot at our next game, and I can't wait to ask Brett if he got to see the front of our house last night. Our tree is so pretty all lit up, but we still need to put the candles in the windows. Can we do that when we get home?"

"Slow down. First concentrate on practice and we'll worry about more decorations if we have time after dinner."

With the door opened, Melanie made a beeline for Brett. Not surprising since that was their routine.

"Brett, did you drive past our house last night? It's all decorated and we even put our tree up in the big window. Momma said you had things to do so you couldn't come over yesterday to help us. But I saved an ornament for you to put on when you come over next time. It's a hockey puck."

He knelt down and gave her a hug. "Hi. You're pretty excited today and to answer the most important question, I did drive by and saw all the decorations, including the tree in the window, and it looks fantastic."

He looked at Jillian and gave her a smile. "Hey."

Her heart constricted. "Hey." She held out her hand. "Come on, munchkin, you need to get ready." She looked away to avoid seeing the hurt in his eyes. She had already gotten a glimpse of it when they walked in.

"Um, did you bring skates? Coach is still out and I could use an extra person on the ice."

Melanie looked from Brett to Jillian. "Momma, they're in the car, remember?"

Well, there was no way she was getting out of helping. As much as she wanted to be close to him, she also needed to keep her distance lest her resolve fail her.

"I'll help."

"Thanks." He checked the laces on his skates. "See you on the ice."

Once Melanie was set, she went to the car to get her gear. Besides being on the ice with the two people she cared about most, lacing up always had a way of giving her clarity. Would it offer her the respite she needed tonight?

As she pushed off to the center of the ice, she found her rhythm. It was like walking, no effort needed. She circled around the perimeter of kids.

"Coach P, what would you like me to do?"

He gave her a grateful smile which made her heart skip. "Can you run skating and turning drills with the Mites A? Work on smoother turns and maybe a little backward skating too."

"You got it. Come on, team A; you're with me." She skated to the opposite side of the rink and the kids clustered around her as if she were the Pied Piper or something.

She explained what they were going to do and broke the kids into groups of four, but out of the corner of her eye, she was watching Brett too. He was a distraction. This was harder than she had expected, but he needed the help.

The rest of practice went by in a blur until Brett blew a whistle.

"Everyone, come over here." Brett waved his hands and pointed to the center of the ice and waited until the kids surrounded him. Parents watched from the sidelines.

"You have all improved so much since our first practice

and with our next game in a few days, I want you to rest up and come excited to play a good game. But remember the most important part of the game is good sportsmanship."

One of the boys raised his hand. "But Coach P, how can you play hockey and be nice? There are fights all the time when I watch the Bruins play the Flyers on TV."

"Sometimes it's easy to forget, but you can play a fair game and if you lose, congratulate your opponent." He gave a stern look to the adults and his eyes came to rest on Jillian.

This was the hardest part of coaching since parents often set a poor example with their antics from the stands. She knew all too well that gracious losing was the toughest part of the game to learn, especially as you got older and the stakes got higher.

In some ways, was this like her relationship with Brett? But a heart was at stake, and that was the hardest part of the body to heal. She knew from personal experience. It had taken years to stop being angry at Danny for walking away from her and Melanie.

Brett said, "Have a good night and see you Thursday for practice."

Melanie glided over to Brett. "Are you gonna come over tonight?"

His eyes met Jillian's over Melanie's head. "I'm sorry, but not tonight. I have some things to get done before..." His voice trailed off. "But I'll see you at practice, okay?"

She turned. "Momma, can't Brett come over tonight too?"

"Munchkin, not tonight."

She looked between the adults and her eyes narrowed. "Are you mad at each other?"

"Of course not. Why would you ask?" Over her shoulder, she said, "Sometimes adults have responsibilities that have to come first." She skated across the ice and reached the door as she finished her sentence.

The look on Melanie's face confirmed her suspicion. She

wasn't buying the line she and Brett were spinning. Jillian was certain she had made the right decision to end things. Melanie was getting too attached.

*T*hey came out of the locker room just as Brett stepped out of the coach's office.

"Well, we're going to hit the road." She gave Brett a look for some support.

"'I'm going to check on Coach Richards. You girls have a good night."

Melanie pushed her hat from her eyes. Her lower lip jutted out and she stomped through the lobby and waited by the exit doors. Jillian knew that look. It was only a matter of time before she would bring up Brett again.

"Sorry about that. She can be a tough little kid."

"I know. If you want to talk later, I'll be home. Give me a call."

With a slow shake of her head, she said, "Brett, I don't think so."

"Why? Because you don't miss me or because you do?"

She groaned. "Of course I miss you, but this is the right thing to do." Her eyes drifted to the ice.

"I disagree." His eyes implored her to change her mind. "Jillian, do me one favor."

She looked up. "What?" Her heart ached so bad, she wanted to rub her chest and try to ease the ache.

"Think about what you really want out of life. I am over the moon about you and your daughter. Why do you want to throw that away?"

Because she wasn't enough for him to want to stay in Dickens. "Good night, Brett."

As she crossed the lobby, she could feel his eyes following her. She wanted to cry but not now, not here, and definitely not in front of Melanie.

"Momma." She jumped on a chair and placed her little hands on either side of Jillian's face. "I love you and you're the best momma ever."

If that were true, then why couldn't she grant the one wish her daughter wanted with all her heart? "It's only because I have the best daughter in the whole wide world."

She gathered Melanie in her arms and covered her face with butterfly kisses until her little girl's giggles put a smile on her face.

CHAPTER 26

*A*fter Melanie was settled in that night, Jillian let the silence wrap around her. Their Christmas tree lights glowed in a rainbow of colors and the silver beads added extra sparkle. Her thoughts drifted back to what Brett had asked. Why would she want to walk away from a man who cared for her and her daughter? How could she hold him in the same realm as Danny?

Brett had lived a life before coming to Dickens. It wasn't like when Danny didn't want to be robbed—his words, not hers—of opportunities.

She got up and turned on some soft jazz. The wonderful strains of Etta James' voice warmed her heart. That woman knew how to sing a song that touched your soul. "At Last" had always been a favorite, but tonight it held a deeper meaning. Was it a sign that she needed to reach out and let the spell of love wrap around her? As the last notes died away, she knew she missed Brett from the bottom of her heart. Love didn't have to follow a timetable or rules. It just was all that it could be: wonderful, scary, and oh-so-worth everything that might come down the road. And she made *her* choice.

She picked up the phone to call him but stopped. Even

though he was open to talking to her, it couldn't be on the phone. It had to be face-to-face so that he really understood her fears and feelings; they went hand in hand. She sent him a text. *Meet me at the gazebo on Wednesday?*

She held her breath and waited for him to answer. The seconds crawled.

YES! He didn't want to wait. Now, that was a good indicator this was the right thing to do. *Five?*

I'll be there.

⁂

$\mathcal{H}$e walked over to the gazebo, where she waited for him. His smile said it all. He was hers. At last, she knew what true love looked like. He was carrying something behind his back. When he reached her side, he sat down.

She tried to catch a glimpse but he moved to block her view. "What's behind your back?"

"Patience."

She placed her hands on his cheeks and kissed his lips. "I'm glad you came."

"I'm glad you called. Is Melanie with your parents?"

"She is at the farm."

His free hand cupped the back of her neck and he pulled her closer, lowering his mouth to hers.

When she was breathless, he looked into her eyes. "Jillian, do you know that it's very hard to buy you flowers since the best place to get them is at Petals? Or I could pick them myself. But"—he swept his hand through the air—"since it's mid-December, there are no wildflowers to be had, which meant I needed a substitute." From around his back, he pulled out a bouquet of holly berries and white poinsettias. "I hope you like them."

The combination of brilliant red of the berries and the

crisp white of the flowers brought tears to her eyes. "This is so thoughtful, but you've done too much. I know it had to be you who decorated the front of my shop with the lights, trees, and birds."

"I had some help; my mom decorated the trees and added the cardinal to represent my dad. John and Heather Gridley helped with the trees and lights, and the doves were from me."

She leaned against the back of the bench. "John and Heather helped? But they're so busy this time of year with the tree farm and her shop, they didn't even take their honeymoon yet."

"He volunteered to deliver a tree and the next thing I knew, we were unloading greens and two trees and Heather pulled out a ladder and we got it done in record time."

"The building has never looked so beautiful."

"It's not more beautiful than the woman who runs the shop. I happen to think the rest of the world is dull by comparison. But there is one tiny confession." He held up a small space between his thumb and index finger. "I'll need to have an electrician come and fix one of the outlets when it gets a little warmer. I'm not overly handy when it comes to some things."

She laughed and held up a hand. "I don't even want to know. But is it like how you tried to make the first few wreaths and they just fell apart?"

"You had to remind me? I only want to revel in the success." He lightly kissed her again. "Can we talk about what happened last week? I don't want there to be any questions about us. I mean that as a twosome plus one six-year-old mini-Jilly."

She took his hand and laced their fingers together. "When Danny walked out on me, Melanie was a few days old. My parents said right from the beginning they'd be there for us, and they've never wavered. I was lucky to start working at

Petals and eventually I bought it. All this time, Danny has provided financially for Melanie but has been absent from her life. He still hasn't called her since he was here. When she told Santa she wanted a daddy, it was clear to me she had chosen you."

"The vanilla ice cream and rainbow sprinkles." He nodded with a small smile. "I don't want to replace her biological father, but I'm confident that I will have my own relationship with her. We already do, and someday I'd like to have a couple of kids with you and be a big, happy family. I'm not asking you now—we have a lot to learn about each other and we'll take this slow, but you're the woman and she's the little girl I see in my future."

"You were right. I needed to really think about what I wanted for my future. I can't help being scared that if something doesn't work out between us, not what it will do to me but what it'll do to all the people we love." She squeezed his hands and searched his eyes. "But I do have an important question. Will small-town life be enough for you? This is very different than life with a professional hockey team."

"I'll answer your question with a question. Do you find this life is enough? You walked away from a promising career in hockey too. Do you wish you had a different life?"

"Not since the moment I knew I was going to be a mom. This is where I want to be."

"I am too." He wrapped his arms around her and held her close. "Never doubt the power of love, Jillian." His lips claimed hers. When he pulled back, he said, "I do love you."

"I love you too." When she looked deep into his eyes, they were filled with love and she knew at last she had found the final piece to make her life complete in Dickens.

"How would you feel about picking up Melanie from your parents and going out to dinner? I'm sure she'd love it, and so would I."

"I'll call Mom and tell her we're on the way."

. . .

*M*elanie was telling Brett about her day at school on the drive to the restaurant. "Brett, are you coming over after dinner to see our tree?"

He turned to look at Melanie. "I think that is a great idea. Do you still have the ornament you wanted me to hang?"

"Yup. A hockey puck." She touched the bouquet on the seat next to her. "Can we get more ornaments? Maybe some holly berries too?"

Brett took Jillian's hand. "I think that can be arranged."

ONE YEAR LATER

Melanie raced ahead of Jillian and Brett as they strolled hand in hand. The ground was covered with a dusting of snow; the air was crisp, and the blue sky was cloudless.

Jillian gave him a huge grin. "I can't believe that in less than two weeks, the construction company will be onsite and our foundation will be dug."

"Well, I'll do you one further. I can't believe that we've been together over a year and we're building our forever home, right here where we took our first Thanksgiving stroll on your parents' land. I remember walking to the pond with you and Melanie to make my wish for the future."

"And you made one this year too. Are you ready to divulge your secret?"

Melanie looked over her shoulder. She had grown tall and every day it struck him how much like her mom she was. Occasionally she'd come out with a phrase or a look that his mom said reminded her of him when he was a boy. Who said family was about sharing the same DNA? It was about love, and he loved this little girl as much as if she shared his last name.

"Momma, you know we can't share our wishes or they won't come true."

He shoulder bumped her. "Yeah. I want all my dreams to come true."

"Mine have," Jillian said.

He couldn't see her eyes behind her sunglasses, but he knew exactly how she felt. It was in the tone of her voice and the caress of her hand.

"I thought while we were out here that maybe we could do a couple shovelfuls of dirt to officially make it our home."

He pointed to a shovel sticking up from the ground. It was where they had said the family room would be and from that vantage point, it looked out over the pond. Even the geese had shown up for the day. It was going to be perfect.

"Melanie, do you want to go first?"

"Yeah, this'll be fun." She frowned. "But we don't have anyone to take pictures."

Brett said, "Yes, we do. I know our parents wouldn't want to miss a moment like this, so I asked them to meet us out here to help commemorate the groundbreaking."

"Good idea," Jillian said. "But it's getting chilly since we're not walking. When are they coming? We do need to get inside to start Christmas Eve dinner."

"Stop being so practical. They'll be along soon. While we wait, let's walk through the floor plan one more time." He had to stall.

"At least it'll keep us warmer."

"For a woman who spent most of her life on ice, you don't like the cold much." He pecked her lips.

"Ha. Without the gear and movement, frosty air is just downright cold." The sound of an approaching UTV drew her attention. "Here they are."

The moms got out of the quad UTV. Dad was carrying a camera.

"Here we are." Alice's eyes were bright. "I can't believe

this time next year, we'll be celebrating Christmas in your new home."

Jean said, "It'll be fun watching the house go up and I'll be close enough so Melanie can ride her bike over."

Roy gave him a long, knowing look and a quick wink. If he hadn't been watching, he would have missed it.

"Alright, Melanie's going first, then Jillian, and I'll finish." He pointed to a spot where the sun wouldn't be staring into their eyes. These pictures would be the most important of their lives up to this point.

He stood behind Melanie. "Don't dig too deep; we just need a bit of dirt."

She held the shovel and tipped out some. It was soft digging.

Jillian said, "Well, that's good. It'll be easier for the bulldozer if the ground's not frozen." She took the shovel from Melanie. "My turn."

She gave the shovel a good push in, but the tip connected with something solid. She looked around and grinned. "Buried treasure perhaps?"

"Back in the day, people used to bury their garbage, so maybe it's something like that," Brett said. "Keep digging. Let's see what it is."

Melanie peered closer. "Momma, look! It's a box! Can we open it?"

She dug around the four corners and lifted it out of the ground, brushing the dirt off with her gloves. The box didn't look that old and there wasn't any rust on it.

"This has been put in the ground recently." She looked at Brett and arched a brow.

He held out his hands. "Let me see."

She handed him the box and wondered what he was up to.

He flipped open the lid. "Another box is inside."

As he withdrew the next box, Mom came over to take the first one. In one smooth motion, he dropped to one knee and popped open the top of a jewelry box.

"Jillian Morgan, last year when you brought me to this spot, I made a wish and today I'm hoping you grant it by agreeing to be my wife and Melanie my daughter. Please say yes and marry me and make all my heart wishes come true."

She threw her arms around his neck and cried, "Yes, yes, yes! I'll marry you!" She covered his face with kisses before holding out her trembling hand.

He slipped a single perfect round diamond ring on her finger.

She turned to Melanie. "Is that okay with you?"

She flung her arms around both their necks and said, "I love you, Momma and Daddy, and Santa granted my wish too. My daddy's favorite ice cream is vanilla with rainbow sprinkles!"

Brett crushed them to his chest and tears flowed down his face. Jillian wasn't surprised by the depth of his emotion. She wiped the river of tears off her cheeks. This moment affected him as deeply as it had her. She held the loves of her life tight.

She kissed him and said, "You have made all my wishes come true today and I'll love you always."

The End

Thank you for reading *Holly Berries and Hockey Pucks*

Please keep scrolling for more books by me.

THANK YOU

I hope you enjoyed the story. If you did, please help other readers find this book:

1. This book is lendable. Send it to a friend you think might like it so she can discover me too.
2. Help other people find this book by writing a review.
3. Sign up for my newsletter by contacting me at http://www.lucindarace.com.
4. Like my Facebook page: https://facebook.com/lucindaraceauthor.
5. Join the Friends who like Lucinda Race group on Facebook

The Crescent Lake Winery Series 2021

Breathe

Crush

Blush

Vintage

Bouquet

A Dickens Holiday Romance

Holiday Heart Wishes

Holly Berries and Hockey Pucks

LAST CHANCE BEACH SERIES

Shamrocks are a Girl's Best Friend
February 2022

The Matchmaker and The Marine

THE MACLELLAN SISTERS TRILOGY
& THE LOUDON SERIES

The MacLellan Sisters Trilogy
Old and New
Borrowed
Blue

The Loudon Series
The Loudon Series Box Set
Between Here and Heaven
Lost and Found
The Journey Home
The Last First Kiss
Ready to Soar
Love in the Looking Glass
Magic in the Rain

•

ABOUT LUCINDA

Lucinda Race is a lifelong fan of romantic fiction. As a girl, she spent hours reading and dreaming of one day becoming a writer. As her life twisted and turned, she found herself writing nonfiction articles, but she still longed to turn to her true passion: novels. After developing the storyline for the Loudon Series, it was time to start living her dream. Clicking computer keys, she has published nine books.

Lucinda lives with her husband Rick and two little pups, Jasper and Griffin, in the rolling hills of Western Massachusetts. Her writing is contemporary, fresh, and engaging.

Visit her at:

www.lucindarace.com
Lucinda@lucindarace.com

Made in the USA
Middletown, DE
10 November 2021